"I don't mean to cause you any grief," Jake said, tilting his head. There was a kindness in his eyes she wasn't used to seeing in a man.

She blinked at him. Flo was right. He was pleasing to the eyes. Inwardly, she shook the thought away. She had no business thinking in those terms.

"I'm not looking for your friendship." She didn't try to hide the exhaustion in her voice. "My coming to your office the other night was misguided. I was desperate. I thought you could help me understand what's going on with my son." Rebecca wrung her hands. "But I suppose that's something I have to work out with Samuel."

The professor put his hand on the railing near hers. For the briefest of moments, she thought he was going to cover her hand with his, warming it.

She ignored the disappointment that swelled inside her when he didn't.

Alison Stone lives with her husband of more than twenty years and their four children in Western New York. Besides writing, Alison keeps busy volunteering at her children's schools, driving her girls to dance and watching her boys race motocross. Alison loves to hear from her readers at alison@alisonstone.com. For more information please visit her website, alisonstone.com. She's also chatty on Twitter, @Alison_Stone. Find her on Facebook at facebook.com/alisonstoneauthor.

Books by Alison Stone

Love Inspired Suspense

Plain Pursuit
Critical Diagnosis
Silver Lake Secrets
Plain Peril
High-Risk Homecoming
Plain Threats

PLAIN THREATS

ALISON STONE

HARLEQUIN® LOVE INSPIRED® SUSPENSE

Recycling programs
for this product may
not exist in your area.

LOVE INSPIRED BOOKS

ISBN-13: 978-0-373-44692-6

Plain Threats

www.Harlequin.com

Printed in U.S.A.

God is our refuge and strength,
always ready to help in times of trouble.
—*Psalms* 46:1

To my son Alex, as you embark on your senior year of high school. May you continue to be fearless and intelligent in your choices. You have the world at your feet, Buddy.
I can't wait to see what you decide to do in life.
I'm so proud of you. Love you.

To my editor, Allison Lyons, who continues to believe in me.
Thanks for your keen editorial input.
My books are the best they can be because of you.

To my husband, Scott, and the rest of my kids,
Scotty, Kelsey and Leah. Love you guys, always and forever.

ONE

"**I** won't be long." Rebecca Fisher scooted forward on the vinyl seat in the van and raised her voice over the swoosh, swoosh, swoosh of the worn wipers scraping against the windshield.

"I have another pickup." The driver's words were clipped, as if a return ride hadn't been understood. He pulled back the sleeve of his jacket and checked his wristwatch. "Meet you back here in thirty minutes?"

"Yah." Gathering the folds of her skirt and her tote bag, Rebecca climbed out of the van, popped up her umbrella and slammed the van door closed. She cast one last glance at the driver, who seemed oblivious to her indecision. Not as chatty as some, the young driver was one of several employed in the heavily Amish community of Apple Creek, New York, to cart the Amish around when they didn't want to be bothered with a horse and buggy.

Standing on the sidewalk under her black umbrella next to the brick building, Rebecca watched the red brake lights of the van as it slowed, then disappeared around the corner. She tugged on her black bonnet, trying to shut out the brisk wind and the whipping rain. It was late September, too early for snow, but the cold and rain were a hint of the winter to come in western New York.

Rebecca checked the address for Professor Jacob Burke on the slip of paper in her hand. Then she squinted at the name of the building carved into the stone above the nearest doorway. Her heart sank. It wasn't the building she was looking for and all the buildings looked the same.

If Rebecca didn't hurry, she might miss the professor. The college student she had talked to at the Apple Creek Diner where Rebecca worked as a waitress had assured her that Professor Burke had office hours on Monday and Wednesday from four until six-thirty.

Rebecca clutched the collar of her coat and turned down the first brick path leading between a row of buildings. *Oh, so many buildings.* A male college student strode toward her, his hands stuffed in his coat pockets, his hood pulled up against the rain and his eyes straight ahead.

"Excuse me. Do you know where…?"

The young man continued past without as much as a sideways glance.

She squeezed the handle of the umbrella tighter and looked down at the piece of paper as it flapped in the wind, the writing smeared from the rain.

"Can I help you?" An older woman stopped and gestured with her umbrella toward the young man who hadn't bothered to stop. "Don't take it personally, dear. The young people today walk around with those thingies—" she pointed to the side of her head "—in their ears. They don't hear anything except whatever it is they're listening to on their phones."

"Oh," Rebecca said, feeling completely out of her element on the college campus. "I'm looking for the Stevenson Building. Room 214. Professor Jacob Burke's office."

"The anthropology building," the woman said, as if suddenly everything made sense. It was no secret the professor of anthropology studied the local Amish. Perhaps the woman thought Rebecca was availing herself to his research, but that was the furthest thing from her mind.

Smiling, the woman spun around and pointed across a wide courtyard with her free hand. "You're close. It's right over there."

"Thank you." Rebecca tucked the piece of paper into the tote she had draped over her arm. Drawing in a deep breath, she pulled back her shoulders and strode across the courtyard to the arched doorway of the brick building. Her pulse whooshed in her ears in competition with the drops pelting her umbrella.

Rebecca pulled open the heavy wooden door and held it for a second with her foot. After wrestling to close her umbrella, she stepped into the marble entryway. The door slammed, echoing in the cavernous space, startling her. She adjusted her wind-whipped bonnet and smoothed what little hair was visible near the crown of her head.

Dragging her fingers along the cool metal railing, she climbed the stairs and walked down the empty hallway until she found room 214. Professor Burke's office.

Slowing her pace, she fumbled with the hook and eye on her coat, feeling the heat gathering. Finally, her trembling fingers released the hook and she slipped off her coat and draped it over her arm. Through the narrow window on the office door, she noticed a young man sitting at the desk and talking on the phone.

Rebecca turned and looked down the hallway; a trail of water had dripped from her umbrella. If she lost her nerve now and left, she'd have to stand in the rain for close to thirty minutes waiting for the driver.

You've come this far.

When Rebecca finally turned the handle and stepped into the narrow entryway, the young man was watching her with a curious expression, something Rebecca would never get used to. Sometimes she wished she never had to leave the farm. She missed the quiet life she'd led before her deceased husband's actions had drawn her into the limelight.

Now most every day she had to venture away from the solitude of farm life to work at the diner, where she often felt like a character in a play, expected to act out a role when the tourists stopped in for a meal. Some even had the nerve to talk really loud to her, as if she were deaf.

However, the end of summer had meant the departure of the bulk of the tourists and their curious gazes. They had been replaced primarily by less generous college students; vacationers tended to leave her an extra dollar or two at the diner after they had tasted her shoofly pie. Money she could ill afford to lose now that she was a single mother.

"Hello?" the dark haired young man said, his lilting voice making it more a question than a genuine greeting.

Rebecca worked her bottom lip. "I'm looking for Professor Burke."

The boy at the desk, who couldn't be much older than her Samuel, turned toward the open door a few feet away. "Is Professor Burke expecting you?"

Under her bonnet her scalp tingled. She had obviously made a misstep. She should have found a way to reach the professor before showing up unannounced.

"I…um…" She smoothed her hand across the coat draped over her arm. The umbrella bounced against her leg when she took a step backward.

"Hello, I'm Professor Burke." A tall, clean-shaven man appeared in the doorway, an inquisitive smile in his warm brown eyes.

Rebecca took a confident step forward but kept her hands securely wrapped around the coat she was carrying, her tote and umbrella clasped underneath. "I'm Rebecca Fisher. I'm Samuel Fisher's *mem*…" She let her voice trail off, hoping he'd acknowledge that he knew Samuel before she went on much longer.

Professor Burke's eyebrows raised and his eyes darkened. "Yes, I know Samuel well. Is something wrong?"

Rebecca felt the young man's eyes on them. "Perhaps we can talk in private?"

"Of course." Professor Burke held out his arm, gesturing to his inner office. When she hesitated, the professor entered his office first and sat behind the large desk.

Rebecca followed him and sat at one of two chairs on the opposite side of the desk. She would have felt claustrophobic in the small space if it hadn't been for the large windows overlooking the courtyard.

The young man appeared in the doorway. "I finished collating the test papers. If there's nothing else, I'm going to blow this joint." His gaze traveled the length of her. Rebecca dropped her umbrella, then she bent over to snap it up, happy for the distraction.

"Thanks, Tommy. Have a good night."

"Night."

The door to the main hallway clicked shut. Rebecca shifted in her seat, relieved to not have an audience. "I'm sorry to bother you this late, but I'm worried about my son. Actually, he was my husband's son, but I claim him as my own." She was telling this man information he already knew.

Professor Burke threaded his fingers and rested his elbows on the desk. She felt as if he was studying her like a farmer inspects a calf before making his bid at the auction.

"I'm very curious why you've come to me, Mrs. Fisher."

"Because I have nowhere else to go."

* * *

"Nowhere else to go?" Jake stood, then walked around to Mrs. Fisher's side of the desk. When he sat next to the young Amish woman, she angled her knees away from him, creating as much distance between them as possible. He looked down and stifled a smile.

"I need to talk to you about Samuel." Mrs. Fisher placed her tote and umbrella on the floor and folded her coat over them. She straightened her back and hiked her chin in a gesture that seemed forced. "I may come across as—" she seemed to be searching for the right word "—*backwoods* to you, but I know you spend time researching the Amish and you know a lot of the *youngie*. You knew Elmer King. And you know my son."

Jake's heartbeat slowed as he remembered Elmer, the outgoing young Amish boy who had died in a car wreck over the summer. The image on the front page of the small-town paper of Elmer King's old red Chevy Camaro wrapped around a tree and his straw hat on the pavement said far more than a tidy quote the journalist had tried to elicit from the professor who studied the Amish. Jake was suspicious that some opportunist had placed the straw hat there for added effect.

A picture is worth a thousand words.

Jake tried to shake the image, but his stomach pitched at his guilt for not having known how to help the boy. Elmer had been one of the youth he had gotten to know over the past three years as a professor at Genwego State. Jake felt strongly that his missteps had led to Elmer racing off in a rage that fateful night.

Dragging a hand across his hair, Jake let out a long sigh, buying time to formulate his thoughts. "Yes, I knew Elmer. What does this have to do with your son?"

"Samuel and Elmer were friends. My son is not the same young man he was before Elmer's death."

"Samuel's had a rough go of it."

Rebecca nodded slowly and wrung her hands in her lap, seemingly growing more agitated. When she didn't seem as though she was going to speak, Jake asked, "How can I help you?"

She gave him a measured stare before dropping her gaze to her hands clutched in her lap. "Professor Burke, I'm worried about Samuel."

Jake rested his elbow on the armrest. He waited for her to continue. As a researcher, he often went into the Amish community and performed a delicate balancing act between developing authentic friendships and fostering relationships in the name of research. It was unusual for an Amish person to stroll into his office, never mind a young Amish woman.

"You've become friends with Samuel and his gang, *yah*?" The Amish referred to the groups of somewhat like-minded young adults who hung around together as gangs. The term lacked the negative connotation that it held in the English world.

"Yes, I've gotten to know your son."

"Is he…" Again, she seemed to be searching for the right word. "Is he okay?"

He studied her face. Myriad emotions played on her features.

"He seems to be okay. I know you both have experienced some backlash from the community after Willard was arrested." Rebecca's husband, now deceased, had been convicted for killing two of his Amish neighbors.

"Backlash." Rebecca seemed to be trying on the word. "*Yah*, we have had issues from graffiti on the barn to smashed eggs on our windows. The sheriff never made any arrests."

"Samuel told me it had stopped." He studied the woman, estimating her to be in her late twenties, early thirties at the most.

"It had. Then more recently, it started up again. Someone took all four wheels off Samuel's wagon…" Her voice trailed off. "I am grateful they took them off and didn't just loosen them. I hate to think—"

"It sounds like a police matter," Jake interrupted. "I'm not sure why you're here… I'm a professor."

Rebecca rubbed her flattened palms together. "It's twofold, really. I called Sheriff Maxwell once… I'm friends with his wife. We grew up together." She waved her hand, as if that part of the story was inconsequential. But any time someone left the Amish community, it scarred those that remained.

Rebecca drew in a deep breath and continued. "Samuel became very agitated when I called the sheriff. He holds himself partially responsible for his father's arrest, even though we all know…well, we all know what his father did."

"Yes, I'm sorry. Sorry for your troubles. Sorry for your loss."

"Me, too. This is not the life I imagined for me or for my children."

"It took a lot of courage for Samuel to work with law enforcement to aid in his father's arrest."

Rebecca ran a shaky hand across her lips. "Maybe he wouldn't be taking this all so hard if his father was simply in prison." Her shoulders rose and fell on a heavy sigh. "When Willard was killed in prison, I think something inside Samuel broke. I don't know how to reach him anymore."

"I'm not sure how I can help, Mrs. Fisher."

"Please, call me Rebecca. I no longer feel like *Mrs.* Fisher."

"Okay…" He hesitated, waiting for her to continue.

"I've watched my son talk to you at the diner. He's confided in you. I need…" She closed her eyes briefly. "…I need to know what you know about my son so I can reach him before I lose him for *gut.* Like the Kings lost their son, Elmer."

Jake ran a hand across his chin. "What is it you're worried about?" A niggling suspicion told him why she was here, but he didn't dare say.

Rebecca's gaze lingered on his. "I need to know if Samuel's involved with drugs like his friend was." Her voice was strained, as if it took every effort to get out the words.

"Samuel's a young adult." Jake measured his response, trying to distance himself from the pain on Rebecca's face. Her son—her stepson, actually—was enjoying his running around years with the usual bending of Amish rules. If Jake broke the young man's confidence, the young Amish men wouldn't talk to him. On the surface, it would jeopardize his research at the college.

"Samuel needs to find his own way," Jake said.

"He needs guidance. He has no father."

Jake didn't know if Samuel was into drugs, but if he was, Jake wanted to be there for him without the interference of his mother. He needed to foster Samuel's trust.

Jake had learned that the hard way.

Rumors spread after Elmer's tragic death. Apparently, Elmer's father had kicked him out of the house after he had learned of his son's drug use. Jake tapped his fingers on his thigh and tried to ignore the familiar ache of guilt eating away at him. Jake had encouraged—no *forced*—the young man to confide in his family believing they would provide the support system the young man needed to straighten up. Instead, his father threw his son out of the house. Elmer fell into a downward spiral. All because of Jake's advice.

"Professor Burke," Rebecca bit out when the silence stretched a little too long. "My son is at a vulnerable time in his life." She lifted a shaky hand to her mouth, then let it drop. "I'm afraid I'm going to lose him."

Jake thought long and hard on how he was going to phrase this. Finally, he said, "I don't know what you want me to do. I thought the point of adult baptism was to allow the young adults in the community to make their own choices."

"It is…" She paused. "It is. But this is far beyond that. Samuel is a different person since his friend Elmer died. He has become withdrawn. He won't even let me in his room."

"Samuel has suffered tremendous loss." Jake leaned his elbow on the arm of the chair. "Be there for him when he comes around."

Nodding, Rebecca reached down and picked up her coat, tote bag and umbrella from the floor and balanced them on her lap, as if ready to spring out of his office. She glanced toward the door. "I hear a lot of things at the diner. About both college students and the Amish doing drugs." She traced the handle of the umbrella. "I fear I'm going to lose him, too."

"Have you asked Samuel if he's into drugs?" Jake angled his head, trying to meet her eye. He found himself fascinated by her wide brown eyes and full lips, sweet and innocent without any hint of makeup.

"Yes." She finally lifted her eyes, deep with worry. "He told me no, but I don't know if I can trust him to be truthful."

Jake settled back in his chair, weighing how much to say. "Drugs and alcohol are an issue in the Amish community, but I don't know if Samuel is involved. You need to talk to your son and keep talking. It's a rough time in a young Amish man's life. He has a tough decision looming ahead of him. He needs your support."

A look akin to disgust wrinkled her nose. "Are you lecturing me in the Amish ways?"

"I'm trying to…" What exactly was he trying to do? Avoid helping her for fear of alienating Samuel? For fear of giving her the wrong advice?

Rebecca held up her hand, stood and took a step toward the door, her frustration evident by her pinched mouth. "I don't know why I thought you'd understand. I'm sorry I wasted your time." Did she suspect he was holding something back?

"Would you have been satisfied if I had told you your son's a drug addict?"

Rebecca eyes flared wide, an emotion straddling fear and my-worst-nightmare-come-true flickered in their depths. "Is he?"

"I have no reason to suspect he is."

"Can you find out and tell me? Maybe he'll confide in you. I have lost much in my life—I can't bear to lose Samuel, too. If he's made a bad choice, I need to help him before it's too late. But I want to do it without getting law enforcement involved. If he ended up in prison…" She shook her head. "I'm holding on dearly to all that I have left."

"I don't want to lose Samuel's trust. I can only encourage you to keep trying to reach him." Jake already knew the devastation of his meddling in Elmer's life.

"Thanks for your time." Rebecca's words came out clipped. She spun around and stormed out of the office.

Jake sat for a moment, replaying the conversation in his head. A subtle thump started behind his eyes. He stood and returned to his chair behind the desk and dialed his assistant's cell phone number. Tommy picked up on the first ring, his voice hushed. "What's up?"

"How much do you know about Samuel Fisher? Is he big into the drug or alcohol scene?" His assistant had grown up in the Amish community and had left to earn his GED and eventually go to college. His background gave Tommy an "in" to the sometimes rowdy *youngie* scene and made him a valuable asset to Jake and his research.

A long pause stretched across the line. For a minute, Jake had thought he'd lost the connection. "Is that who that Amish lady was? Samuel's *mom*?"

"Yes."

"And his *mem*—" the word sounded foreign on Tommy's lips, mocking almost "—thinks he's into drugs and alcohol? Is that why she stopped by?"

"She's worried about him." Jake absentmindedly doodled an *R* on the piece of paper in front of him and traced over and over it. "She wants to know what I know about him."

Tommy laughed. "Far as I know, Samuel's a good kid. I'd vote him most likely to bend a knee before he's twenty-one."

"Yeah? You really think he'll choose to be baptized into the Amish community?" Jake felt reassured. "Rebecca Fisher seems to think he might be in some kind of trouble."

"Nah, not Samuel." A rustling sounded over the line, like from a gust of wind as if he were still walking.

"Aren't you home yet?"

Tommy laughed. "What? Are you my keeper? I had some errands to run." Wind muffled his words again. "Let

Mrs. Fisher know Samuel's a good kid. He's not into drugs or anything. Not as far as I know."

"She'll be relieved."

"Hey, anything else?" Tommy asked. "I have to run."

"No. Thanks." Jake ended the call and tossed aside the pencil. He stood and grabbed his coat from the hook. If he hurried, he might catch up with Rebecca.

Give her some good news for once.

Rebecca ran down the hall and out the door. Behind her, the heavy door slammed shut, like all her hopes of reaching her son. She stopped short and blinked against the soft mist of rain as she fumbled to open her umbrella. She strode forward, deciding getting wet was the least of her problems.

She had tried everything. Absolutely everything. The professor had been her last hope to uncover what was bothering her son. At the diner, she had noticed how comfortable Samuel seemed chatting with the professor. She had hoped he knew something that would help her reconnect with her son or at least intervene if the professor could pinpoint her son's troubles.

But this not knowing… This was more painful.

Maybe the professor did know something and he wasn't sharing.

Even if he did, what could she do with the information? Samuel paid her no mind.

A strong wind whipped around her long dress and her thick stockings underneath. Not for the first time, she muttered evil thoughts about Willard. He was destroying his family long after his death. The leaves on the trees rustled in the wind, setting her nerves on edge. She released her coat from her tight hold and stuffed one arm, then the other, into the sleeves, juggling her tote bag and umbrella. She ran, fighting back the tears.

She couldn't lose Samuel. His little sisters would be devastated. *She* would be devastated.

She swiped at the tears.

She hadn't realized how tightly she had clung to this last measure. To the notion that Professor Burke would help her.

As a young married woman, Willard had isolated Rebecca and she had felt increasingly alone. She had been ruined when she realized the father of her children was a murderer. But she had never felt more alone, more wrecked, than she felt right now. She could never reclaim her place in the Amish community if she lost both her husband and son to the evils of the outside world.

Her family would never be *gut oh tzene*. No one would ever respect the Fishers again.

Rebecca had heard rumblings at the diner that someone was dealing drugs in town and it might be one of the Amish *youngie*. Her insides ached every time she thought of it. She had no proof that Samuel would do such a thing, but his complete change in character made her imagine the worst. Sure, he had lost his friend, Elmer, but Samuel had been through far worse. Or maybe it was the culmination of everything he had been through that had put him in the pit of despair.

Would the professor have told her if he had heard Samuel was dealing drugs? She hadn't dared to ask him *that* question. She was fiercely protective of her son.

Rebecca stopped to catch her breath and her bearings. Her chest heaved. Blinking, she looked around. She didn't know how long she had been in Professor Burke's office. She only hoped the driver she had hired was waiting for her.

The building in front of her looked unfamiliar. Long

shadows darkened her path. Suddenly, she realized the country college campus was deserted except for a couple girls walking away from her, their heads angled close in conversation. A hollow feeling expanded inside Rebecca. She missed her friends. Willard had seen to it that she didn't have any, both before and after his death.

And here she was alone and…lost. In the rain. Where had the van dropped her off? She had been in such a tizzy when she'd left the professor's building, she hadn't paid attention to her surroundings.

Stupid woman! Willard's voice rang in her head. She shook it away. Willard couldn't control her anymore.

Rebecca strained to see if she could hear the idling of a motor, but all she could hear was the wind whistling through the leaves clinging to the branches.

Rebecca turned on her heel and strode back the way she had come, then made a sharp right near the professor's building. Now that she had calmed down, she recognized the bench next to a brick memorial.

Yes, she had passed this way.

Only a little farther to the main road where her driver should be waiting.

Her heartbeat returned to normal.

The shadowed brick path wandered between campus buildings.

Just a little bit farther.

Crash. The sound of exploding glass sounded over her head. Instinctively Rebecca ducked against the rain of glass fragments.

Squinting, she lifted her head. Someone was running toward her. A dark shape. Adrenaline made her blood run cold.

Dear Lord, watch over me.

The person stopped near her, the face impossible to

make out in the heavy shadows under a large hood. When the person lifted an arm as if to strike her, Rebecca cowered and tiny explosions of light danced in her line of vision. Her eyes darted around, searching for an escape.

"Leave me alone," she said, her voice squeaky with fear. Instinctively she held up her umbrella in a defensive gesture.

Get to the van!

"Rebecca!" She glanced over her shoulder, a wave of relief slamming into her. *The professor.*

She spun back around and the mysterious person had slipped down a dark alley between two buildings.

Professor Burke caught up to her. "Did you know that person?"

She shook her head, unable to find the words. She held the umbrella down by her side as the rain hit her fiery cheeks.

"Are you okay?" He placed his hand at the small of her back and gently guided her toward his building. Once inside the doorway, he closed her umbrella, then helped her out of her coat. He stepped outside and shook the glass off it over a trash can.

When he stepped back inside, Rebecca finally found her voice. "I think he intended to strike me. He raised his hand. If you hadn't called my name..."

Compassion shone in his warm brown eyes. Rebecca lowered her gaze. The professor touched her shoulder. "Wait here."

Rebecca put her coat back on, then stood inside the entryway for what seemed an eternity while the professor ran back outside. When he returned he shook his head as concern creased the corners of his eyes. "Someone smashed the light."

"Why?"

The professor rubbed the back of his neck. "You've been harassed before. Because of Willard."

Cold fear rained down on Rebecca. "W-w-we've had the incidents at the farm. The graffiti on the barn. The eggs smashed on the window. Nothing physical. The community was lashing out after what my…what Willard Fisher did."

The professor scratched his head. "Did anyone know you were coming here to see me?"

Rebecca struggled to keep the threatening tears at bay. "I was talking about it at the diner. I suppose anyone could have overheard me." A chill skittered down her spine. "I thought time would make things better. Not worse." She hugged her coat around her midsection. "Do you think that's what all this is about? Willard?"

"I wish I knew." The compassion in the professor's voice warmed her heart. He held out his arm, drawing her farther into the building. "Let's call the sheriff." The professor pulled his cell phone out of his pocket.

Her mouth went dry and she shook her head briskly. "No. I'm not hurt. I don't want to complicate things. I want to go home."

The professor hesitated a moment, then much to her relief put the phone away. He seemed to regard her a moment. "I came looking for you to tell you my assistant believes Samuel's a good kid."

She studied his face. "What does that mean?"

"My assistant is former Amish. He hangs out with the young men. More than I do, even. He thinks your son is a good kid and likely to be baptized."

Her eyes flared wide and hope sparked in her heart. Had she heard him correctly?

"Some of the men in his gang are a little wild. I've seen it firsthand, but that's not unusual," Professor Burke added.

"Maybe I can get him to switch gangs." Samuel had

picked his current buddy bunch when he'd turned sixteen. His group of friends was mostly composed of youth his age. But maybe…

"Maybe." The doubt in the professor's eyes unnerved her.

"Uri and Jonas, the brothers helping out on my farm, are in his gang. Maybe I should question them." She hadn't done this for fear of embarrassing Samuel in front of his friends and pushing him further away. "Samuel is not himself. I don't care what your assistant says."

Silence stretched between them.

"Let me drive you home," the professor offered.

"But my driver…" She didn't feel much like arguing; her nerves were too frazzled.

"Do you have his cell phone number? I'll call him."

She handed him her hired driver's business card. She'd call him from the diner whenever she needed a ride. The professor paused a moment when she handed him the card.

Rebecca wanted to cling desperately to the hope the professor had offered her. *Samuel is likely to be baptized.* But deep in her heart she knew something was wrong. Very, very wrong. She had once heard her friend Hannah describe it as a mother's intuition.

Rebecca feared Samuel was being consumed by the dark shadow his father had cast upon his family.

Rebecca shuddered. She feared that she, too, would forever stand in the dark.

TWO

The wheels of Jake's truck made a rhythmic thrum-thrum-thrum noise on the road. He usually cranked tunes whenever he was in the car, a surefire method to drown out his thoughts. However, he doubted Rebecca would appreciate his penchant for classic rock. And singing along.

Rebecca shifted in her seat, partially facing him. "I appreciate your kindness in driving me home." She tapped her fingers on the seat next to her, as if working up the nerve to say something. "I'd appreciate if you left any mention of our conversation out of any publications."

A sharp dagger twisted in his gut. Jake had prided himself on respecting the Amish and portraying them in the best possible light. But as a professor, he always built off the facts. He never twisted his findings to suit his hypothesis.

"The newspaper quoted you in the paper after Willard's arrest," she said accusingly when he didn't answer. "You shouldn't have mentioned me or my children."

"I only mentioned your family in brief. I focused on Willard. You have to appreciate how curious outsiders would be."

"All too well. Unfortunately, curiosity didn't stop with the outsiders," Rebecca muttered.

A muscle ticked in Jake's jaw. "Please forgive me for being blunt, but that was a fascinating case. It rarely happens that an Amish person commits murder." He had respected her privacy. He had seen the sadness in her eyes and he would have felt like a vulture—like nothing more than a bloodthirsty journalist hot on the trail of a story—if he had approached her for an interview. Instead, he was careful to feed the news media facts regarding the Amish. It was only logical considering his position at the university and his proximity to Apple Creek.

"While you hide behind your fancy job at the university, I'm stuck living the life of a murderer's widow. How do you think people look at me in town? It's not like I can avoid their curious stares. I had to get a job at the diner to make ends meet."

"The Amish community is known for their forgiveness." Here he was spouting out his Amish research to her, an Amish woman. He did realize the ridiculousness of it, but he was struggling for something to say.

"Many have been kind, but I see the looks of pity in their eyes. It's painful. A few have acted out…like perhaps tonight."

"The sheriff wasn't able to get any leads on the previous incidents?"

"No," Rebecca whispered, "but once we stopped calling the sheriff, the number of incidents died down. I thought we were in the clear."

"Do you suspect your Amish neighbors?"

She shrugged. "It's hard to imagine…any of this, really."

"Now you fear if Samuel leaves the Amish community, the judgment from your neighbors will be unbearable."

"The look when I gaze into a mirror will be unbearable. I want my old life back. Before Willard lost his way."

Jake adjusted his grip on the steering wheel. "I'll be there for Samuel as much as he allows me to be." Samuel had grown quieter of late with him, too. "Maybe he's struggling with his decision to remain Amish."

"He is acting out. Hanging around with boys who drive cars, skipping out early on church service, listening to loud music…" She let her words trail off, perhaps hoping he'd confirm the list or perhaps add to it. "Maybe his friends are leading him astray."

"Perhaps."

Rebecca huffed her frustration. "Samuel has not had the typical Amish upbringing. His mother died when he was a young boy. He had an overly strict father who was killed in jail after his murder conviction. That, I fear, has shaped him more than anything. More than any positive influence on my part."

"My interviews with Samuel show he was confident that testifying against his father was the right thing to do."

"After his father's death…" She stopped to compose herself, then continued, "…Samuel retreated away from everyone. Then this summer, after Elmer's death, he got worse. Far worse. I'm afraid soon I'll have lost him for *gut*."

She faced him squarely. "Perhaps you can talk to him about his father? I can't bear to do it. You could convince Samuel that he did the right thing. By stopping his father, he undoubtedly saved lives." Hope laced her soft voice.

"I can." Jake turned up her driveway as dusk gathered. He thought he saw a light go off in the basement. Maybe it was the reflection of his headlights in the uneven glass of the narrow basement windows.

"I have built a solid relationship with Samuel and a group of other young Amish men. I can talk to them. I'll encourage him to come to you. But I must be cautious about how much I reveal. They are young adults. He's at the age where he needs to be making his own decisions. Living his own life. And dealing with consequences on his own."

Rebecca unbuckled her seat belt and pushed the door open a fraction. She bowed her head, leaving him studying the top of her bonnet. "Thank you." She twisted to get out of the car.

"Let me walk you to the door."

She held up her hand in refusal.

"The house is dark." Now he was second-guessing himself. Had he seen a light snap off in the basement?

"Samuel is…out." The statement seemed more a question. "My daughters are visiting my brother, Mark, spending the night. I'll turn on a lamp once I get inside. I'll be fine."

"Are you sure? The incident on campus must have rattled you. I think we should've called the sheriff."

"*Neh*, I want to put the night behind me. We've had enough trouble out here."

Jake pushed his truck door open. "I'm escorting you to the door."

"*Neh.*" Rebecca shook her head for emphasis. "I've been on my own for well over a year now. I don't need a man to walk me to the door. I'm not looking to bring more trouble into my life. If Samuel trusts you and is talking to you, I want that to continue. You're right. I shouldn't have interfered. And—" a shy smile tilted the corners of her mouth "—I don't want to give my neighbors another reason to gossip." Rebecca ran her fingers down the ties of her bonnet. "You can find me at the diner if there's anything about Samuel you feel you can share."

Jake stared at her for a long moment, then pulled his door closed. "Okay." Her dismissal had been unmistakable. "Please turn on a light once you get inside. I'm not leaving until you do."

Without saying another word, Rebecca climbed out of the car. In the growing darkness, he watched her move toward the farmhouse, her full skirt swinging around her legs. He had spent three years studying the Amish youth, but he had never had a conversation like he'd experienced tonight.

Rebecca's dark hair and dark eyes would stay in his memory long after her clean scent left the cab of his dirty old pickup truck. Completely against his nature, he waited in his truck drumming his fingers on the steering wheel, while Rebecca let herself in.

He watched as she disappeared into the house and he waited.

And waited.

As time stretched, his pulse thudded in his ears. No light.

"Come on, Rebecca."

He angled his head and leaned closer to the windshield, as if that would make the light appear sooner. He glanced at the digital clock on the dash. Three minutes had passed.

Shaking his head, he pushed open the car door.

Something was wrong.

Rebecca unlocked the front door and stepped inside. She locked the door and placed the keys on the small shelf next to the door. The scent from last night's fire in the wood-stove still hung in the air. Growing up, the smell always had made her feel warm and cozy, the sign of an inviting home in the cold of winter. That had been a long time ago. Too much in her life had changed since the tranquil days of her childhood.

Back sore, she set her tote bag and umbrella down on the bench inside the door.

When she had met Professor Burke she hadn't expected such a warm gentleman. Some of the Amish elders, although polite, had complained about the so-called professor meeting with their youth and filling their heads with worldly ideas.

However, Rebecca wasn't sure. She thought the professor was truly interested in studying their way of life, not inserting himself into it. However, she couldn't hide her disappointment that he couldn't give her any new information about her son. She had hoped to find a way to reach Samuel because she had failed at all her attempts and Samuel only seemed to be growing more distant with time.

She took off her coat and hung it on a hook. Maybe it was the nature of being a young man on the cusp of making a pivotal decision in his life.

Oh, she wouldn't be able to bear it if he left Apple Creek. She feared for his soul if he did.

A rattling sounded at the back of the house. Maybe it was Samuel. What if it wasn't? A quiet yelp sounded in her throat and she almost called out to him when something made her pause.

Holding her breath, she walked through her home toward the kitchen. The floorboards creaked under her deliberate steps. The back door yawned open and a stiff wind sent it crashing against the wall.

A dark shadow bolted across the yard. Tingles of panic bit at her fingertips.

Someone had been in her house.

Rebecca slammed the back door shut and turned the key in the lock. How had they gotten in?

Her raspy breaths sounded in her ears. A pounding at

the front door startled her. She spun around and stared, uncertain what to do. She was out here. Alone.

Slowly, she walked to the front door. Her mouth grew dry and a weight bore down on her chest, making it difficult to breathe. She reached the front door and flattened her hands on the cool wood.

"Who is it?" The words came out as a croak.

"It's Jake. Are you okay?"

Relief washed over her. With a shaky hand, Rebecca grabbed the keys and opened the door. All her limbs went numb. Her lips couldn't form any words.

"I got worried when you didn't turn on a light." The professor's gaze swept across the sparsely furnished room cloaked in heavy shadows. Rebecca wondered if he saw something she hadn't. Rockers sat in the middle of the room. A table with her knitting sat between the chairs. The familiar setting seemed foreign now.

An intruder had been in her home.

Rebecca crossed the room and turned the switch on the kerosene lamp, casting the room in a warm yellow glow. She couldn't stop shaking. "Someone was in my house. They ran out the back door when I came in."

The professor stepped back, the surprise evident on his face. "Are you sure they're gone?"

Rebecca's eyes drifted to the back of her house. "I s-s-saw s-s-someone running across the yard." She clamped her jaw to get it to stop shaking.

"I need to check the house. Make sure no one else is here."

Her stomach dropped to her boots. Why hadn't she thought of that? She grabbed the arm of the rocker and lowered herself into it, suddenly feeling sick.

"Stay close to me while I check the house." The professor held out his hand and she studied it a minute before rising to her feet and taking it. A knot of emotions trapped her words. "Do you have a flashlight?"

Nodding, she dropped his hand and led him to the kitchen. She grabbed the cool handle of the solid flashlight sitting on the counter and handed it to him.

Its beam made everything not in its path seem even darker. The professor must have sensed her discomfort. "I'll make sure you're safe."

A nervous giggle escaped her lips. "Yeah, the professor protecting an Amish woman."

The professor moved toward the basement door. "Don't underestimate me. Before I went back to college for my PhD, I was an army ranger."

"I suppose that makes you tough?" She had heard of the army, of course, but she didn't know what a ranger was. The Amish were conscientious objectors and didn't believe in fighting in wars.

The professor opened the basement door and cast the beam of light down the stairs. "Tougher than most." He gently squeezed her hand. "Stay right here. I'm going to check the basement."

After a few long, tense-filled minutes, he emerged from the basement. "No one's down there. Let's check upstairs."

She nodded, nerves getting the best of her.

As she skulked behind the professor, afraid to walk through her own home, she could already hear the church elders tsk-tsking over a man who wasn't her husband going upstairs. Surely they'd understand. *If* they ever found out. Right now, the elders weren't her biggest concern. Someone hiding under her bed or lurking in a dark corner was.

Fear knotted her stomach. She'd never be able to sleep tonight.

The professor pointed his chin toward the door at the top of the stairs. "Is this your bedroom?"

She nodded and emitted an indecipherable sound that she hoped he took as yes. She lingered in the doorway as the professor made a sweep of the room. *Empty.* He did the same in the room Grace and Katie, her young daughters, shared. She was grateful she had left them with her brother, Mark, and his family for the night. They were only six and eight and Rebecca wanted to provide as much consistency for them after everything they had been through in their young lives.

The last upstairs bedroom was Samuel's. He kept the door shut. He had been doing that for the past few months, ever since Elmer had died. Rebecca immediately felt traitorous for letting this stranger into her son's room. A room her son didn't even allow her access to.

The professor gave her a quick nod, his face heavily shadowed in the hallway. He turned the handle and pushed the door open.

Rebecca skirted around the professor and turned on the kerosene lamp on the bedside table. She sucked in a gasp. The room was a mess. The quilt she had personally made for Samuel was askew on the bed. Papers littered the floor.

"Samuel hasn't allowed me in here for months."

A battery-powered radio sat in the corner, and an assortment of silver disks littered the floor around it. She walked over to the closet and picked up a thin laptop and turned it over in her hands. She willed away her nausea as she met the professor's gaze. "I had no idea he had this." She held up the computer in her hand. Before her job at the diner, where people came in to work for hours on these things at some of the best tables near the windows, she wouldn't have known what it was. "I have no idea how he'd afford a laptop. Why would he need this?"

The professor slowly strolled the perimeter of the room. Was he mentally cataloging her son's belongings as if his room were an exhibit in a museum? Her mouth grew dry. Feelings of betrayal welled up again. Why had she allowed this man who made a living studying the Amish into her son's bedroom?

"Please don't use this in your research. This is my family's private business." She didn't want to give the church elders reason to not allow her son into the preparation classes for baptism next summer.

Her heart filled with self-recrimination. She should have never brought an outsider into her life. *Their* lives.

The professor finally spoke. "You didn't know he had all these things?"

Rebecca shrugged. "I didn't want to know." She lowered herself onto the corner of the bed. "It's not uncommon for the *youngie* to explore worldly things. I hoped after his father, he would have been less likely to stray."

"You suspected something was going on. That's why you came to me." She tried to read the question he wasn't asking. Did he now suspect Samuel of dealing drugs? How else would he have earned the money for these things? Slowly blinking, Rebecca wished she hadn't listened to her gut. Wasn't she happier before she knew what her husband was really up to? The same could be said for her son.

What did she really know?

Rebecca smoothed her fingers along the edge of her cap and nodded. "I can't lose him. I can't. My daughters would be devastated."

I would be devastated.

"Do you notice anything missing?"

Rebecca lifted her head and looked around. "In here? I wouldn't know."

"What about in the rest of the house?"

"I don't think so. I have nothing of value."

"Maybe they wanted something your son had."

Rebecca's gaze swept across the room, a room completely foreign to her.

The professor pulled his cell phone out of his pocket. "I have to call the sheriff. Report a break-in."

"You can't." Desperation made her chest tight.

"I don't understand. Someone was in your house." He stopped and turned to face her. "Do you know who it was?"

Rebecca shook her head. "Of course not."

"I'm calling the sheriff."

Rebecca watched as the professor dialed the number, then lifted the phone to his ear. She was helpless to stop him.

Rebecca had made a huge mistake.

Rebecca sat ramrod straight in the rocker across from the professor as they waited in the sitting room for the sheriff to arrive. She was kicking herself for approaching the professor. She should have kept everything in her family private.

Now look what they uncovered in Samuel's bedroom.

And if she hadn't wasted time going to the university, she wouldn't have given the intruder an opportunity to break in.

Willard's cruel, mocking voice scraped across her brain. *Stupid, stupid woman.*

Neh, neh, neh! She was not *that* woman anymore. She was strong. She had to be.

If you are so strong, why is Officer Maxwell on his way over here to nose into your business? The Amish are supposed to stay separate. In this world but not of this world. You're going to screw things up and lose Samuel now. It wonders me how you'll ever be respected by the Amish.

Rebecca squared her shoulders, trying to shake her husband's mocking words free from her brain. She realized her argument was flawed. The intruder could have made his way into her home while she was there. Then what would have happened? She could have been hurt or worse.

The memory of the man advancing on her on campus flashed in her mind. Were these events related? Had graffiti and egg-throwing veered toward more dangerous personal attacks? Would the community never forgive her for Willard's horrid acts?

If this even had to do with Willard.

Rebecca rubbed her temples, hoping her headache would ease. She dropped her hands and frowned. Better to cloak her growing fear in annoyance. Easier to cast the blame of her predicament onto the professor. However unfair.

Rebecca wasn't in the mood to admit it, but calling the sheriff was the practical thing to do, even if unorthodox for the Amish.

Footsteps sounded on the porch, followed by a brisk rap at the door. She started to get up. The professor was faster.

Sheriff Maxwell looked past the professor toward her. "Everything okay out here, Rebecca?"

She sighed softly and shook her head. She and the sheriff weren't strangers. He had been instrumental in making sure her husband was behind bars. Rightfully so, but his presence was a painful reminder of a part of her life she'd rather forget.

The sheriff's gaze slid over to the professor and Rebecca felt foolish for ever believing a stranger in her life was a good idea. "You know Professor Burke."

The sheriff opened his mouth but closed it again. Perhaps he was going to say something that had crossed Rebecca's mind.

Why was he here?

Instead the sheriff held out his hand. "Hello, Jake. What's going on here? You said Rebecca had a break-in?"

The professor nodded. "Rebecca returned home and saw someone running out the back door."

"Anything taken?" the sheriff asked.

"Not that I can see." Rebecca ran her hands down the skirt of her long dress. The professor's watchful gaze unnerved her.

"Where's Samuel?" the sheriff asked, glancing around.

Rebecca's eyes grew wide. "He's not home." She couldn't help but bristle.

"Do you know where your son is?"

"It wasn't Samuel, if that's what you're thinking. He wouldn't have run away from me." Did she know that for sure? Hadn't he been moving away from her for months? She swallowed hard. "Samuel's a young man. I don't need to keep track of his every move." Yet that's exactly what she had hoped to do by contacting the professor.

The sheriff nodded, as if he were considering this. "If nothing has been taken, I'll write up a report and keep an eye out for any suspicious people wandering around tonight. Make sure you keep your doors locked."

Rebecca nodded again, feeling queasy. Many residents of Apple Creek had added locks to their doors after the tragic murder of her friend and neighbor. The locks had been useless in keeping the murderer out of her home. Rebecca had been married to him.

"There's another thing, Sheriff," the professor said.

Rebecca spun around and glared at him.

"Rebecca was almost attacked on campus. I'm afraid if I hadn't come along when I had, she would have been hurt."

She wanted to deny this, but...she couldn't. Nervous tingles danced up her arms. In one fell swoop, she had brought two outsiders into her life: the professor and the sheriff. She closed her eyes briefly. If Samuel got wind of this, he'd distance himself further.

She'd lose him forever.

"What happened?" Sheriff Maxwell asked.

Rebecca explained the glass on the lamppost exploding above her head and the man advancing on her. Icy dread pumped through her veins as she finished the story.

"Do you think this is tied to the previous harassment?"

Rebecca lowered her gaze and heat infused her cheeks. The sheriff had been out to her farm after the graffiti and egg-throwing incidents, even though Samuel had begged her not to call the police. He claimed it would only aggravate the situation. But Rebecca had feared for her family's safety. Someone had to stop them. But no one had. The perpetrators were never found. So Rebecca had stopped bothering the sheriff. Eventually things died down, until recently.

"Have you had any interactions at the diner that made you feel uncomfortable?" the sheriff asked, his tone compassionate.

"It's quiet at the diner this time of year, mostly college students and locals." She cut a sideways glance to the professor, wishing she could read his mind.

"You've had some help on the farm?"

Rebecca glanced up to find the sheriff studying her closely.

"Yes, Uri and Jonas Yoder. They've been a tremendous help. We wouldn't be able to farm the land without them."

"Any chance it was either of them in your house tonight?"

"*Neh...*" Her tone was less than confident, but she hoped the sheriff didn't pick up on it. She needed the Yoder brothers to harvest the crops. They were the sons of a well-respected Amish couple with ten children. They had been happy to offer their sons to help her in her time of need in exchange for minimal pay.

"Rebecca, if you think of anything else, you know where to reach me," the sheriff said.

She nodded.

The sheriff headed toward the door, then turned back again. "Hannah and I would love to have you over to the house for dinner. The girls would love to play with Katie and Grace."

Rebecca folded her hands in front of her. "That would be nice." For her daughters. For her, seeing Hannah brought back painful memories. Rebecca's husband had killed Hannah's sister and brother-in-law, leaving Hannah to care for her two nieces in Apple Creek, separate from the Amish community. Rebecca and Hannah had been dear friends as children, a lifetime ago.

A stomping sound on the porch drew all eyes to the door. Rebecca's heart sank. Samuel burst into the house. Under his broad-brimmed straw hat shadowing his eyes, she had a hard time discerning if he was angry or afraid.

Samuel took off his hat and ran his hand over his blunt-cut hair. "What's going on?"

The more her son hung around with the *youngie*, the more he sounded like an *Englisher*. It was as if the young Amish were all trying to shed their Amish roots.

"When I came home someone was in the house."

Samuel's gaze wandered to the stairs, perhaps thinking of his bedroom.

Oh, Samuel, please talk to me.

"Who was it?" Samuel's words were clipped.

"I don't know. He ran out the back. Did one of your friends stop by?"

Samuel scratched his head, leaving a tuft of hair sticking up. *"Neh."* Glancing at the sheriff, then the professor, he lowered his gaze. "I don't think so."

"I'll stop by the Yoder farm. See if the young men are home," the sheriff said.

Samuel's eyes grew wide. *"Neh. Mem*, why would you bring these outsiders here? Don't we have enough trouble being accepted among our neighbors after what *Willard* did?" He used his father's given name to distance himself. What son wanted to admit his father was a murderer?

Rebecca's knees grew weak. "My son is right. That will only stir up more trouble. The Yoders are *gut* boys."

The sheriff hesitated a fraction, as if he were thinking it over. He then clapped Samuel's shoulder. "Good to see you, son. Keep an eye out for your *mem* here and be sure to call me if you guys see anything suspicious." The sheriff was savvy enough to know most of the *youngie* carried cell phones during Rumspringa. It was frowned upon, but the elders turned a blind eye to it, hoping the young people would bend a knee when the time came.

"Good night, Sheriff," Rebecca said, eager to see him leave.

She closed the door behind him, then rested her backside against it. "Is everything okay, Samuel?"

Her son narrowed his gaze at the professor. "Are you friends with my *mem*?"

The professor seemed to be searching for the right thing to say. "I hope we can be."

Samuel's nose twitched as if he were trying to process the scene. Rebecca's heart pulsed in her ears. She didn't want to push Samuel away by revealing she had gone to the professor to try to exact information out of him.

Apparently sensing this, the professor spoke up. "I gave your mom a ride home." An apologetic smile slanted his lips. He had told a lie of omission, obviously leading her son to believe he had given her a ride home from the diner. "Then all this craziness broke out."

"Oh." Samuel stared straight ahead, skepticism written on his face. "I'm going to bed." He stomped up a few stairs before Rebecca called to him.

"Do you know anything about what happened here tonight?"

Samuel stopped without turning around. "How would I know? I wasn't home."

Rebecca caught the professor's eye. Unease twisted her insides, worrying how far she'd push Samuel.

"You must be tired."

Samuel nodded curtly. "*Yah*, I'm going upstairs." Samuel continued his stomp up the stairs like a petulant child. When he reached his room, he hollered down the stairs. "Who was in my room?" He thudded down the stairs, his chest heaving.

"I was in your room." Rebecca approached the bottom of the stairs. "Where did you get all that stuff?" The walls of the house seemed to sway as she waited for the answer.

Samuel pressed his lips together but didn't say anything.

Rebecca worried about the consequences of talking in front of the professor, but she was overwhelmed. She couldn't let this defiance from her son slide a minute longer. "Where did you get the money for a computer?"

A muscle ticked in Samuel's jaw and suddenly he looked like a man. An angry man. "Stay out of my room," he spat out.

"Samuel, your mother's worried about you." The professor moved next to her, making her feel like for once she wasn't alone.

"*You* don't have to worry." Samuel ran upstairs and slammed the bedroom door.

Rebecca and the professor exchanged worried looks. Samuel was definitely hiding something.

THREE

The next afternoon at the diner, Rebecca grabbed the whipped cream can she could see through the glass door of the refrigerator and yanked off the cap. Lost in thought she squeezed the trigger on the dispenser and watched the white cream ooze out into a hearty dollop on two pieces of apple pie.

Drawing in a deep breath, she picked up the plates and turned her back to push through the swinging door leading to the dining room. The door swung back with a swoosh on its hinge, and she delivered the two pieces of pie to the elderly couple in the booth by the window.

"Can I get you anything else?" Rebecca asked.

"No, dear," the older woman said, "thank you." The couple came in at least once a week and Rebecca couldn't help but envy the easy way they chatted and held hands over dessert.

As Rebecca retreated to the counter, the elderly gentleman muttered something about how delicious the pie was.

Flo, the waitress on duty with her, pulled the filter basket out of the coffeemaker and turned it upside down over the garbage. With a gentle tap on the edge of the can, the wet coffee filter and used grounds slid into the garbage.

Flo was in her sixties and she was a fixture at the diner

as much as shoofly pie and apple butter. People might have thought she was Amish because she wore her long gray hair in a bun at the nape of her neck and her plain gray waitress uniform might have passed for Amish to the average tourist.

But Flo was *not* Amish. She had *English* sensibilities and had raised three boys, now grown. She freely shared advice with Rebecca whether she wanted it or not.

Flo spun around, planted her fist on her hip and smiled. "Still worried about Samuel?"

"I…um…" Rebecca muttered, embarrassed that she had been caught daydreaming and not getting her work done. She grabbed the dishtowel from the back counter and wiped down the already clear countertop. There was usually enough going on in the small diner to keep both waitresses hopping, but now just so happened to be the short lull between lunch and dinner.

"Well, I didn't figure you were staring at me because you forgot how the coffeemaker worked," Flo said with a funny smile. "What's on your mind?"

Rebecca twisted the rag in her hands. "I went to see Professor Burke last night." Rebecca didn't have many Amish friends of late and she appreciated the friendship of the older woman. Rebecca missed her Amish friends, her family. Her parents had long since moved to an Amish community in Florida for health reasons and her friends had disappeared as Rebecca's troubles multiplied.

Flo raised a pale eyebrow and regarded Rebecca for a long moment. She was a solid Christian woman, but she had a wicked sense of humor that could make Rebecca blush. That knowledge, coupled with the glint in her eye, had Rebecca bracing herself for the older woman's reply.

"Professor Burke is a very handsome man." Flo twisted her lips as if considering something. "Too bad he's not

Amish or you're not English. You'd make a striking couple."

Rebecca smoothed a hand across the edge of her bonnet, feeling her cheeks heat. None of her Amish friends spoke this boldly. "It has nothing to do with that. I wanted to talk to him about—"

"You know who he reminds me of?" Flo grabbed a fresh filter and used the orange scoop to put fresh coffee grounds in the coffeemaker.

Leaning her hip against the counter, Rebecca didn't bother to answer because she knew Flo would get to it in her own sweet time. Before meeting Flo, she had never been around a woman who said whatever was on her mind. The Amish women Rebecca had grown up with were far more reserved.

The older woman snapped the coffee basket back into place and turned to face Rebecca. "You know who I'm talking about, right? Professor Burke reminds me of that really handsome FBI agent who works with that Bones lady."

Confusion creased Rebecca's brow. "Excuse me?"

Flo's face lit up and she laughed, waving her long fingers in front of her. "Sometimes I forget you don't watch TV." She shook her head. Flo grew serious and stopped doing busy work, giving Rebecca her full attention. "I'm sorry. Tell me why you went to see Professor Burke."

Rebecca glanced toward the dining area to make sure no new customers had come in. She didn't want anyone to overhear. The only patrons were the elderly couple by the window, and they seemed content to chat over their pie and coffee.

"Samuel and some of the other Amish youth meet with Professor Burke for research purposes. I wanted to see if he could help me understand why Samuel has been withdrawn lately."

"How so? Did he tell you something about Samuel that you didn't want to hear?"

"No, but when he drove me home—"

"He drove you home?"

"He was being nice." Rebecca decided to leave the part about being attacked on campus out of the story. "Someone was in my house when I got home."

"Oh, dear." Flo leaned forward and cupped Rebecca's elbow. "Who was it? Are you okay?"

"I'm fine." Rebecca shook her head. "I don't know who it was. The intruder ran out the back door. Professor Burke called the sheriff."

"The sheriff will track him down, I'm sure of it." Flo tried to buoy Rebecca's mood with her optimism.

"The only problem is that the Amish try to limit their interaction with law enforcement."

Flo squeezed Rebecca's elbow and gave her a reassuring smile. "Sometimes calling the sheriff can't be avoided. You know that."

A guilty heat burned Rebecca's stomach. Would everyone always remind her of her horrible past?

"I'm trying to help Samuel—not get him into more trouble."

The lines around Flo's eyes deepened in confusion. "I don't understand why calling the sheriff would affect Samuel."

Rebecca bowed her head. "I shouldn't be bothering you with all my troubles."

"You need to share or—" Flo lifted her hands to both sides of her head, then flared her fingers "—or your head will explode."

"Well, the professor wasn't able to give me any new

information about Samuel's bad mood. When the sheriff arrived last night, Samuel was rude to him. I don't need my son to be on the sheriff's bad side."

Flo's expression softened. "I'm sorry you're having troubles, but maybe it's time you stop smothering that boy." She laughed, a sharp sound. "A boy. Listen to me. He's a man. He could vote if he was so inclined. Stop trying to make him fit into a certain mold." She lifted her finger and tapped the side of her head. "He's got his own ideas."

Rebecca blinked slowly, realizing her English friend wouldn't understand.

As if reading her mind, Flo said, "I'm a mother, too. I raised three boys. My husband was convinced that one of them would become an engineer like him." She rolled her eyes and shook her head. "One became an accountant, another a policeman, and the last—much to my husband's distress—took up creative writing. Poor kid can't afford to pay attention, but my husband, God rest his soul, finally had to realize each of his sons had their own path in this life."

An ache Rebecca couldn't define filled her.

"The Amish are not like the English. We don't seek personal fulfillment. We are community-centered. God-centered."

"Is your son happy?"

Rebecca flinched. "That is not—" She stopped herself, realizing her friendship with Flo was more important than slamming her over the head with how the Amish culture is different from the outside world.

"I realize the Amish march to a different beat, but Samuel is his own person. If he's not happy, something has to change."

Rebecca didn't do well with change.

The bells on the diner door jangled, startling her. Rebecca's friend and the sheriff's wife, Hannah, strolled through the door with her young niece Sarah.

Flo leaned in close and whispered, "Hannah Maxwell seems happy since she left the Amish."

Rebecca walked away without comment because she couldn't find the words.

Hannah lifted her hand and waved. She placed her hand on her niece's bun. "Sarah had ballet class in town and we thought we'd stop by and say hello. How are you?"

Rebecca smiled, feeling a little less lonely. Hannah had stopped by because she was married to the sheriff and she knew Rebecca was struggling right now.

"I'm doing fine." Rebecca smiled at Sarah, admiring her hair, thinking that not that long ago the little girl had been wearing a bonnet and long dress, not a leotard and a pink bow. This was before Hannah had come back to town to care for her deceased sister's children and had fallen in love with the sheriff.

"We're going to start practicing for the Nutcracker," the little girl said. "I'm hoping to be one of the sugar-plum fairies."

"Christmas is still months away." Rebecca met Hannah's gaze.

"They start practicing early." Hannah unzipped the front of her niece's jacket. "Maybe you can color for a few minutes while I talk to my friend Rebecca."

Sarah slid into a nearby booth and Rebecca gave her a child's paper place mat and three crayons. "Hope you like red, blue and green."

"Thank you," Sarah said, picking up the red crayon and following the maze path on the place mat.

Hannah moved toward the counter and Rebecca followed. "Spencer told me he saw you yesterday."

Rebecca's eyes widened. Embarrassment heated her cheeks.

Hannah waved her hand in dismissal. "My husband doesn't bring his work home. He's a good sheriff. He keeps his business confidential, but I sensed that you might need a friend to lean on." She tilted her head to look into Rebecca's eyes. "You okay?"

Rebecca sat on the edge of a stool and crossed her arms. "Don't you sometimes wish we could go back to when we were all little girls? You, me, your sister. Collecting things for our hope chests."

Hannah's eyes grew red-rimmed and she gave Rebecca's arm a squeeze. "I miss my sister every day." She sniffed. "Nothing turned out like we had planned." Hannah's lips curved into a thin smile. "But that doesn't mean some things can't turn out okay." She glanced in the direction of her niece. "I love my sister's daughters like my own and Spencer is a good man. I found light at the end of a very dark tunnel."

Rebecca feared the light at the end of *her* tunnel was a flickering pinprick in danger of being extinguished.

Rebecca squared her shoulders and pushed off the stool. "I'm going through a rough patch, but we'll be fine."

"I'm here if you need me. Please don't be a stranger."

"Denki." The Amish word for thank you came easily when chatting with her old friend.

"Well, we need to pick up Emma from her friend's house and get home." She reached out and patted Rebecca's hand.

"Come on, sweetheart," Hannah said to her niece. Sarah scooted out of the booth clutching the place mat.

Rebecca watched Hannah and Sarah walk hand in hand toward the exit. Hannah glanced over her shoulder. "Don't hesitate to call." She jerked her head toward the phone mounted on the wall, indicating Rebecca could call her from the diner if she needed her. "You don't have to go through any of this alone."

Rebecca nodded. Hannah seemed happy outside the Amish, so why did the thought of her son leaving the Amish fill her with unbearable sadness?

Because leaving meant walking away from everything Rebecca firmly believed. It wasn't about happiness in the moment; it was about faith and God and heaven.

What would happen if Samuel left?

Rebecca ran a hand over her forehead. The beginning of a headache was pulsing behind her eyes.

"Excuse me." The elderly lady seated at the window booth snapped Rebecca out of her reverie. "Could we have more coffee, please?"

Rebecca tugged at the edge of her apron, embarrassed that she had been inattentive. "Of course." She spun on her heel and strode toward the coffeemaker.

Flo came out of the back and gave her a sympathetic smile. "You've got the weight of the world on your shoulders, honey. You need to let go and let God."

Rebecca smiled in spite of herself. Flo's outward expressions of faith were contrary to her Amish upbringing, but she appreciated the sentiment all the same.

She had to have faith.

A tiny bit of the weight lifted from her shoulders. She grabbed the coffee and strolled over to her only customers.

A few nights later, Jake pulled his pickup truck—a vehicle that had seen better days—over to the edge of the road in front of the Troyers' farm. The sun had already set and the final remnants of light were making their last stand. An unpainted split rail fence separated the property from the country road. Beyond the house, barn and a few small structures, corn grew for miles.

Jake pushed open his truck's door and climbed out. He flipped up his collar, hunched into his coat and shuddered. He'd grown up in this part of the country, but he'd never get used to how quickly summer's heat turned to fall's cool evenings.

Jake had stopped by the diner this afternoon. He had been disappointed that he hadn't run into Rebecca, but he had gleaned some useful information. He'd overheard the Troyers had hosted church service this morning, which meant they were hosting the youth singing now. Jake hoped he had timed it correctly to catch some of the *youngie* as they were arriving. He wanted to talk to Samuel, in part to clear up any misunderstanding as to why he was at his home the other night. He didn't want to jeopardize his relationship with the Amish youth. Outwardly, it would hurt his research and his position at the university, but more important, he wanted to be in a position to help Samuel if he had gotten caught up in something. If Samuel pushed him away, he wouldn't be able to help.

Jake's failure to help Elmer would haunt him forever.

Jake wanted to see firsthand why Rebecca was worried about Samuel. To date, the young men he had talked to had not given him cause for major concern apart from the normal shenanigans of an Amish male prior to baptism. But the sheriff's concerns about drugs in the Amish community made him wary.

And Rebecca's plea for help wouldn't allow him to let this go.

The tiny stones on the driveway crunched under his brown loafers. Singing flowed out from the barn. The event must have started earlier than he had thought. As he got closer, he noticed a few Amish boys leaning against a buggy, the red glow of cigarettes lighting up with each puff like fireflies setting the night aglow.

Hands stuffed in his pockets, Jake approached them, scanning their faces. *No Samuel.*

"Ah, it's the professor. So nice to see you," one of them said. Even with the Pennsylvania Dutch accent, Jake recognized the universal language of sarcasm.

Jake knew the youth. Eli Troyer. Apparently being the host family for the singing didn't mean he felt obligated to sit through song after song from the *Ausbund*.

"Sorry to crash your party," Jake said, trying to sound nonthreatening.

Eli tossed his cigarette on the gravel and snuffed it out with the tip of his boot. Uri and Jonas Yoder, Rebecca's farmhands, watched silently, puffing on their cigarettes. Jake wondered how Eli's father felt about finding all the cigarette butts around the barn after the Amish youth descended upon his home.

"What's up, Professor? You looking to take notes? Count how many cigarettes I've had? Rat me out to my *mem*?" Eli gave him a pointed glare, narrowing his lips and emitting a steady stream of smoke.

Jake ignored the comment. "I'm looking for Samuel."

Eli adjusted his hat farther back on his head, the soft light from the barn lit on the amusement in his eyes. "Didn't you get enough information from his *mem*?"

One of the Yoder brothers laughed, a monotone sound that lacked amusement.

"I told you my research was private. That I protect your identities unless you give me permission to use your names."

Eli tapped out another cigarette and put it between his lips without lighting it. The crunching sound of footsteps on gravel grew closer. Samuel strolled around the corner.

His eyes widened a fraction at seeing Jake, but he quickly composed himself, shoved his hands under his armpits and exuded an air of aloofness. "What are *you* doing here?"

"I wanted to talk to you."

"I'm done talking."

"Because I talked to your mother?"

Samuel pushed the gravel around with the toe of his boot. "Exactly. You didn't keep your end of the bargain. I talked to you for research for some stupid paper you had to write on the wild Amish youth." In the heavy shadows, Jake couldn't see it, but he sensed an eye roll accompanying the word *stupid*.

"My research is important." But not as important as the welfare of this young man.

"Not to me."

Uri, Jonas and Eli laughed at their friend's witty comeback. It was as Jake feared. However, securing his research subjects was only part of the reason he had driven out here tonight. The other was concern for Rebecca's safety. Someone obviously had something against her and wasn't ready to let it go. He had heard rumblings throughout the Amish community that not everyone believed Rebecca was blameless. He had heard one young man repeat the ramblings of his father. "It wonders me how a wife couldn't know what her husband was up to. She's just as guilty, I tell you."

Then there was the issue of drugs in Apple Creek and Rebecca's concerns that perhaps Samuel had gotten himself involved.

How had he paid for all the electronics in his room?

Like a research puzzle, Jake wanted to snap all the pieces into place in hopes of discovering what was going on here before any more lives were ruined.

"Can you give me a few minutes, Samuel?" Jake tipped his head toward his truck parked on the side of the road. "I can give you a ride home. It'll be a lot warmer than riding in a friend's buggy. Unless, of course, you brought your own buggy." Jake glanced around but couldn't determine how Samuel had gotten here.

Samuel glanced down, studying the gravel. "I'm going to the singing."

"We both know you have no plans to join the group."

"The professor got one thing right." Uri playfully punched Samuel in the arm. "But my friend here ain't going with an *Englisher*."

Jake caught Samuel's eye; a mix of defiance and fear flashed in their depths.

Jake pulled the zipper on his jacket up to his neck, blocking the brisk fall breeze. "Can I ask you guys something?"

Eli leaned back on the buggy and rested the heel of his boot on the wheel. The other three youth looked at him with apparent disinterest.

"The sheriff told me there are a lot of drugs flowing through Apple Creek."

Eli grunted and crossed his arms over his chest.

"You guys know anything about that? Heard about anyone dealing?" Jake jerked his chin toward the crops. "Heard of anyone growing marijuana?"

Uri laughed. "Yeah, we'll be selling marijuana at the roadside stand next to corn and pumpkins."

Jake turned to Samuel. "How about you?"

Samuel kept his expression neutral. "The only drug stories I hear are the ones that make the papers." *Like Elmer's tragic accident.* "Sorry…" He shrugged. "Can't help you."

They stood staring at one another, silent save for the youth singing in four-part harmony in the barn.

Eli pushed off the wagon wheel. "Let's get out of here. This singing is a drag tonight." Eli gestured to what Jake thought was the buggy with an overabundance of reflector decals, but actually, he was looking past the Amish form of transportation to a ten-year-old beater car Jake hadn't noticed before. "Let's leave before my *mem* brings out snacks. Then we'll be forced to join the group."

"Samuel?" Jake asked, a hopeful note in his voice.

"I gotta go, man." Samuel turned his back to Jake and followed his friends. The four of them got into the car, Uri behind the wheel. The engine roared to life and the worn tires spit out gravel before the treads finally gained purchase and the car tore out of the yard.

A couple horses lifted their heads and snorted in protest. Jake watched the red taillights disappear into the dark night.

Jake wondered if his father had been this rebellious before he convinced Jake's mother to pack it up and leave everything that she'd ever known for a life on the outside.

Stuffing his hands in his pockets, he hunched his shoulders and strolled slowly to his truck. The sweet, dry scent of corn reached his nose, making him feel nostalgic for a life he had never known. Maybe it was simply because it was in his roots. His genes. Would studying the Amish and teaching a new group of students an Intro to the Amish course each semester ever satisfy his need to connect with his ancestors?

"Whoa!" An Amish boy hollered to his horse as he tugged on the reins, quickly swerving around a distracted Jake.

Jake jumped out of the way and waved a hand in apology.

The buggy came to a stop in the gravel lot. "Hey, Professor, if you're not careful, you'll end up in one of those research papers of yours. How the Professor Got Run Over by an Amish buggy."

Jake rolled his eyes and laughed. "I'll pay more attention next time."

"It's best that you do." The young man hopped off his buggy and walked around to tend to his horse.

Jake nodded and strode to his truck. He feared he had ticked off a few of his research subjects tonight. His gut told him that was the least of his concerns.

After church service Rebecca had spent the day visiting her brother, Mark, and his family at their farm about a mile from her home. She always had a hard time around her brother, his wife and their five children. *That* was supposed to be her life, too.

She had never anticipated leading the life she did.

Rebecca had spent longer than she had planned at Mark and Gloria's house because her daughters were enjoying the company of their cousins. She hated to pull them away too soon. It warmed her heart to see them laughing, carefree… belonging.

After the girls climbed into the buggy, Rebecca wrapped a buggy blanket around Katie, then helped Grace pull hers up around her shoulders. Her youngest smiled and shuddered, her breath turned into a puff of white. "It's too cold. Can't we sleep at *Aenti* Gloria's house tonight?"

"You have school tomorrow."

Her sister-in-law, Gloria, danced on the balls of her feet, white breath forming on a sigh. "Oh, let them stay. We can get them to school in the morning with my children. What's two more?"

Rebecca hesitated. "You've been too kind to me. They've been here much too often." It would be easier to leave the girls here in her brother's warm house. She felt her resolve slipping.

"The cousins enjoy each other. Let them stay," Gloria said.

"*Yah*, you're right." Rebecca turned to her daughters. "Girls, would you both like to stay?"

Katie and Grace scrambled out of the back of the buggy and jumped one at a time onto the ground while holding Rebecca's hand. She planted a kiss on each of their foreheads. "Now mind your *aenti* Gloria." She lifted her gaze to her sister-in-law. "I'll pick them up after my shift at the diner tomorrow evening?"

"Perfect." Gloria turned around and, with a hand to each of their backs, she guided Rebecca's daughters into the warm, cozy house.

Something about watching her daughters walk away made a cloak of sadness settle around her shoulders. She let out another breath and climbed into the buggy. A stiff wind whipped up, refocusing her attention to the mile-long journey. Alone in the dark.

Rebecca had been foolish to stay late. She flicked her wrists and Buttercup lurched forward. She'd be home in no time, she reassured herself.

Buttercup trotted down the country road. The lampposts cast lonely rings of light every couple hundred feet or so. If Rebecca wasn't careful she would doze off behind the reins. Buttercup had traveled this road enough; she could easily make it back to the farm without much guidance from her.

Rebecca didn't care for traveling at night, but it did have one advantage—there weren't many cars on the road.

As if to prove her wrong, a car crested the hill and whizzed past her traveling in the opposite direction. That was always preferable to cars driving too close on the same side of the road.

With the car gone, Rebecca let her mind drift to what

she'd do when she got home. Without the girls at the house, it would be lonely. Maybe she'd go into Samuel's room while he was at the Sunday-night singing. She hated to snoop, but she had been shocked to see his stash of electronics. Radio. Laptop. And she knew he had a cell phone. She feared she had already lost him and that his presence at the house was merely out of necessity because he had nowhere else to go.

She wondered how Willard would have reined in his son, then she quickly dismissed the thought. A year had passed since his arrest and she still shuddered at the thought of her husband's cruelty.

Buttercup neighed and Rebecca's attention snapped back to the road. Sensing a car coming up behind them before Rebecca did, the horse instinctively pulled over closer to the edge of the road into the buggy lane. The car sped past them, too close. Rebecca squinted after the red taillights, suspecting it was the same car she had seen going in the other direction only moments before. Her nerves buzzed. A young woman out here alone on a backcountry road was vulnerable.

Stories of buggies colliding with cars made the local paper all the time. She gave the reins a gentle flick and Buttercup picked up her pace.

I'm almost home. Dear Lord, keep me safe.

When the bright red brake lights of the car came on, the tips of her fingers tingled as she tightened her grip on the straps. She made a noise with her lips and snapped the reins. The horse picked up her trot.

The car slowed and made a wide U-turn, its wheels crunching on the berm of the road. Rebecca shielded her eyes against the bright headlights as the car raced back in her direction. A knot twisted her insides, much like it had every time Willard returned home and she'd feared his mood, his outbursts, his angry demands.

Let them drive by. Please, let them drive by.

She flicked the reins again, her eyes locked on the approaching car. At the last minute, the driver swerved into her lane, playing a deadly game of chicken.

Buttercup spooked and took off like a shot, veering closer to the ditch. The buggy's wheel dipped into the deep ditch lining the country road. The sharp motion tossed Rebecca out of her buggy.

A yelp escaped her lips.

It seemed like an eternity as she flew through the air. She landed on her side with an oomph. Her hip and shoulder sank into a few inches of cold, mucky water. Panic made a flush of goose bumps race across her skin. She groaned and struggled to her feet, the wet folds of her dress weighing her down.

Buttercup stopped a ways down the road and neighed his protest. Somehow the buggy had stayed out of the ditch and rested on the side of the road, seemingly no worse for wear.

Thank you, Lord.

Searching her dark surroundings, Rebecca paused and listened. The hum of the vehicle grew distant. Relief, mixed with fear and anger, created a steady pounding behind her eyes. She planted her hands on the cold, hard-packed dirt on the edge of the ditch.

She wiggled her toes in her wet boots.

She struggled to pull herself up but couldn't gain traction. She feared whoever stumbled across her in the light of day would find her, feet frozen in the icy water.

Gravel crunching under tires made the fine hairs on the back of her neck stand on edge.

Had they come back for her?

Rebecca leaned against the edge of the ditch, her palms pushing into the dirt, hoping her black coat in the black of night made her invisible.

Still hitched to the wagon, Buttercup neighed, obviously stressed over the near miss.

A car's engine idled behind her buggy. A door opened. Closed. Rebecca's entire body trembled from the cold. If whoever had returned didn't kill her, hypothermia would.

Footsteps sounded on the gravel. Growing closer. Closer.

Adrenaline surged through her veins. She had nowhere to hide.

She pressed her cheek to the ditch's edge, trying to make herself small. Invisible. The smell of earth and moisture filled her nostrils.

A man loomed above her and Rebecca bit back a scream.

FOUR

"Are you okay, ma'am?" Jake couldn't keep the alarm from his voice. He crouched on the side of the road and stretched his hand out to the woman in the ditch. "Let me help you."

The woman tilted her face up and the moonlight glinted in her worried eyes. "Rebecca! What in the world happened?"

Rebecca squinted up at him, her lower lip trembling. "S-s-someone spooked Buttercup and she dumped me out of the buggy."

Jake twisted and looked down the road. No one in sight. He wrapped his hand around her chilly fingers. "Let's get you out of there and warmed up before you freeze to death."

He immediately regretted his choice of words.

Rebecca gathered up the wet folds of her skirt in one hand and tightened her grip on his hand with the other.

He pulled, but instead of tugging Rebecca out of the ditch, he found himself losing his footing on the muddy edge of the ditch. Rebecca's wet hand slid out of his and she flailed back and landed with a whoosh on her backside in the water. She closed her eyes, briefly stifling the words to match the look of disgust on her face. "*This* is your plan? Hmm…"

"Whoa…hold on. Step back." The water swooshed around her boots as she stepped out of the way. "I'm going to have to try something else."

Before he had a chance to overthink it, Jake jumped into the ditch next to her. The shock of the cold water shot through him. His leather loafers weren't exactly traipsing-in-icy-water gear. He looked down at her and thought he detected a smile on her lips in the moonlight.

Jake assessed the situation. "I'm going to have to hoist you out of here from behind."

Her lips slanted, indicating her skepticism. "Behind?"

"Trust me," Jake said, grimacing as the cold water sloshed around his loafers.

"I dare say you haven't given me *gut* reason to trust you yet."

"Rebecca," Jake said, feeling more than a little out of his element. "You're going to have to work with me on this before we both catch hypothermia out here." He lifted one foot, then the other, unable to escape the frosty pain.

Rebecca nodded, her lower lip trembling.

"On the count of three, I'm going to give you a shove partway out of the ditch. You'll have to pull yourself up the rest of the way."

Rebecca nodded, her bonnet askew on her head; a long strand of silky brown hair had escaped her bun. He bent over and threaded his fingers together. Put your foot here and I'll boost you up and over the side."

Rebecca gave his hands a you've-got-to-be-kidding look, but she lifted a small foot and stepped into his clasped hands. With one quick push-shove-hoist from Jake, Rebecca was able to grab hold and get to her feet on the side of the road.

"How are you going to get out?" Rebecca wrapped her arms around her middle and loomed over him, the moon haloing her bonneted head.

Jake had maintained his physical fitness since retiring from the army by working out at the campus gym. Now was when all that exercise would pay off. He hoped. He found a foothold on the wall of the ditch and was able to pull himself out rather quickly.

Jake followed Rebecca over to Buttercup. She smoothed her hand down the horse's mane and whispered soothing words to the animal.

Rebecca finally turned to him, a look of fear in her eyes. "The car intentionally swerved in front of me. They spooked Buttercup." Her lips trembled. "I..." She patted Buttercup's mane. "We could have been killed."

"Could you describe the car?"

Rebecca shook her head slowly. "It passed a few times before it came at me."

"Any chance it was an older car? Three or four guys in it?" He thought of the vehicle Samuel, Eli and the Yoder brothers had hopped into.

"I don't know. The lights blinded me. But it was a car, not a truck like you have and not a van."

"Do you think it was random?"

Rebecca shook her head. "No, I think the driver knew exactly who I was. That's why he drove past a few times first. He wanted to scare me." She slurred her words, her lips numb.

Would Samuel really allow his friends to harass his mother? Risk seriously injuring her and her horse? Or worse?

Samuel didn't strike him as that kind of kid. Jake shoved a hand through his hair. The last conversation he'd had with the young men crossed his mind.

"Come on. You can't stand out here. I need to get you home." Jake gently took her by the elbow and led her to his truck. "You need to get inside. Warm up."

Rebecca pulled away. "I can't leave Buttercup here."

"No, no, of course not. I'll call my assistant. Tommy's comfortable with horses."

"No, I don't live far. I'll get her home." She strode back to the buggy, the folds of her wet dress slapping her legs.

Jake followed her. He reached into the backseat and grabbed a thick blanket. As he wrapped it around her shoulders and pulled it tight at her neck, his knuckles brushed against the cool, smooth skin of her jaw. She looked up at him with something in her eyes he couldn't quite define.

Rebecca clutched the blanket and climbed into the buggy. "I'm happy you happened along. Thank you for s-s-saving me." She nodded to him dismissively.

Jake laughed. "You really think I'm going to let you ride off alone? You're freezing. I need to see you safely home."

A look of confusion swept across her features. Jake hopped into the buggy and nudged her aside with his hip. "Give me the reins."

Silently, Rebecca handed him the leather straps. "What about your truck?"

"I'll pick it up later."

"Do you know what you're doing? Have you ever done this?"

"I'm an army ranger—I'll figure it out. If I get it wrong, you can tell me."

Even though he knew that wouldn't mean much to Rebecca, he thought he detected a smile on her quivering lips.

"S-S-Samuel won't be too happy to see you and me together again."

Jake raised his eyebrows but didn't say anything. Samuel was exactly who *he* wanted to see.

* * *

When the professor flicked the reins, Buttercup lifted her head and neighed, jolting forward and stopping.

"I think she's still a little spooked from the run-in with the car." Instinctively, Rebecca reached out, her hand brushing his hand as he held the reins a little too tightly. "Let me."

The professor hesitated a minute, then scooted over a bit, making it easier for her to take control of the horse. "I guess I'm more an 'insert key and turn, press gas pedal' kinda guy."

She cut a quick glance to this man, a stranger, really, who spent his time studying her community. Her neighbors. Her son.

The brisk autumn breeze ruffled the edge of the blanket draped over her shoulders. One side slid down behind her back. The cold from her wet skirt seeped into her undergarments. She stifled a shudder. Soon she'd be home and she could light the fire. Put this dreadful night behind her.

Buttercup trotted down the road, the steady, familiar clip-clop-clip calming her nerves.

"This is the first time I've been in a buggy," the professor said.

"Really? I thought with all your research, you would have had the opportunity before now."

He shrugged. "No. Maybe someday when we're not all wet and cold you can show me how to do it."

"Do what?"

"Show me how to get Buttercup to follow my commands."

"There's nothing to it, really," Rebecca said, heat warming her cheeks. "It's a matter of trust. Buttercup has been a wonderful horse." She had taken the animal in when Hannah had moved away from the farm with Sheriff Maxwell.

Rebecca tightened her grip on the reins. "In my world, I don't have the option of 'insert key and turn, press gas pedal,'" she said, mimicking him.

He laughed, the sound pleasant after such a rough evening.

"I remember the first time I saw an Amish buggy." The professor's voice seemed nostalgic. She waited for him to continue.

"I was traveling through Lancaster County, Pennsylvania, with my parents and there they were, one buggy after another traveling on the side of the road. I couldn't believe it."

"What couldn't you believe?"

"That people would actually choose to live without…" He seemed to be searching for the right word so as not to offend her. "…All the modern conveniences."

"You can't miss what you never had." She gently tugged the reins to direct Buttercup toward her barn. The buggy bobbled over the ruts in the mud.

"At the time, I must have been around ten, I was fascinated with a certain TV show and I couldn't imagine not being able to catch the next episode."

Rebecca smiled to herself. Just the other day Flo had told her how the professor had reminded her of a character on one of her TV shows. Who was it? She wondered if he'd find it flattering.

The professor hopped off the buggy and jogged around to help her down. She had plenty of practice doing it all on her own, but it was nice to have a helping hand. Willard had been gone a long time now.

On the second floor of her house, she noticed a soft light glowing in Samuel's bedroom. A mix of relief and fear tangled in her belly.

Samuel spent far too much time in his room. What was he doing?

"I'll get Samuel to settle Buttercup for the night." Rebecca stopped by the porch steps, a little unnerved that Professor Burke seemed insistent on seeing her to the door. "Thank you for coming to my rescue." She gripped the railing tighter.

"I'll have Samuel take you back to your truck," she said, eager to go inside.

The professor glanced down the road. "No, I can jog back. It's not that far."

"But you must be cold, too." She noticed the bottom of his wet pants. The leather on his shoes was discolored from the water. "Those don't look like running shoes."

He shrugged. "Actually, I would like to talk to Samuel before I left."

Rebecca bowed her bonneted head and looked up at him shyly. "Can I ask you a question?"

"Shoot."

"Why are we so fascinating to you?" She grabbed the blanket and pulled it tighter around her shoulders.

"The Amish?"

She nodded.

The professor ran his hand over his close-cropped hair. "My parents grew up in an Amish community. They were Amish."

She jerked her head back. "Really? How interesting. They left the Amish community." It was more a statement than a question.

"It was my father's idea and since my mother loved him, she followed him." He lifted his eyes, the moonlight glinting in them, making it hard to read the emotion there. "My father always joked, calling them fence jumpers. My mother always bristled at the comment." There was something sad about his tone.

"So, Professor, is this why you study the Amish?"

He smiled that warm familiar smile. "Partly." His answer came out clipped and she felt as if she had stepped out of bounds. "I think it's time you called me Jake. We've spent a lot of time together."

A smile tugged on her lips, but her feelings of fondness were fleeting. An empty road stretched behind him. And beyond that, her Amish neighbors.

The line of connection snapped as reality slammed into her. The last thing she needed was the neighbors chatting about poor widowed Rebecca Fisher entertaining the English professor. Her Amish neighbors would be requesting not to sit in her section at the diner in a silent form of protest. A shunning of sorts. The Amish's unique way of guilting a person back into the fold. Back into following the church's rules.

"I'd rather call you Professor." The ever-present uneasiness tightened its grip on her chest. Would she ever be able to move past the shame her deceased husband had created? It was a physical pain she doubted she'd ever be rid of. If only she and Samuel could find acceptance in their own community. If only the Amish could dig deep into their vast well of forgiveness and bestow it on her.

"I don't mean to cause you any grief," Jake said, tilting his head. There was a kindness in his eyes she wasn't used to seeing in a man. Willard had been cruel.

She blinked at him. Flo was right. He was pleasing to the eye. Inwardly, she shook the thought away. She had no business thinking in those terms.

"I'm not looking for your friendship." She didn't try to hide the exhaustion in her voice. "My coming to your office the other night was misguided. I was desperate. I thought you could help me understand what's going on with my son." Rebecca tapped the railing, a nervous gesture. "But I suppose that's something I have to work out with Samuel."

The professor put his hand on the railing near hers. For the briefest moment, she thought he was going to cover her hand with his, warming it. She ignored the disappointment that swelled inside her when he didn't.

She had experienced a riot of emotions tonight and suddenly she felt extremely tired. And cold. So very cold.

"I can respect that," the professor said, a gentleness to his voice. "However, I'd still like to talk to Samuel tonight before I go."

Rebecca glanced toward the door of her house. "I don't know." Her meddling seemed to only cause more problems.

The professor bowed his head, then looked up and met her gaze. Apprehension settled in his eyes. "I know you don't want to hear this, but I think Samuel might have been in the car that ran your buggy off the road."

The blanket fell from her shoulders and her body swayed. *"Neh."*

Rebecca's face grew white and her lower lip trembled. Jake grabbed her elbow to steady her. "Let's get you inside. Where it's warm."

She yanked away her elbow. *"Neh*, I'm fine." He understood her anger, but he wasn't going to let it stop him.

"What's...what's going on?" Samuel stepped onto the wide porch and rushed to his mother's side. "Are you okay?"

She spun around and pointed at her son. "Go inside, Samuel. Professor Burke is leaving."

Then Rebecca straightened her shoulders. "Please." She softened her tone. "Go inside. It's been a long night."

Samuel's gaze implored her. "Did something happen?"

"Do you know what happened?" Jake watched the young man closely. In the year since he'd been meeting with Samuel, the boy had gone from quiet and reserved to angry and fearful. He had assumed Samuel's attitude change had to do with his friend Elmer's death. However, as the harassment on the farm and toward Rebecca continued, Jake began to wonder if something else was at play.

Samuel looked everywhere but at Jake.

"Do you know something?" Jake asked again.

Samuel ran his hand up and down one suspender and stared at his boots for a moment too long. "I have no idea what you're talking about." Samuel turned to his mother. "What happened? Did you have an accident?" His gaze ran the length of his mother's dress, no doubt searching for assurances that she was all right.

"A car spooked Buttercup. I was thrown from the buggy."

Samuel shed his defensiveness and a worried expression crossed his features. He looked much younger than his eighteen years. His gaze drifted to the street, then he seemed to school his expression. "You shouldn't have been out this late." He glanced around; renewed fear pinched his mouth. "Where're Katie and Grace?"

Rebecca touched her son's arm. "They're fine. They stayed with *Aenti* Gloria."

"Were you in the car that spooked the horse?" Jake asked, carefully studying Samuel's expression.

Worry settled in Samuel's wide eyes. He pushed his straw hat back farther on his head. "No. No, I wasn't," he said adamantly.

Rebecca stepped closer to her son. "I know you weren't in the car with them, but you need to be careful. You know the community is still watching us after—"

"After my *dat*." Samuel pulled away from his mother. "Don't you think I know that?" His eyes narrowed. "Is that all you care about—what other people think?" He held out his open palm. "You were tossed in a ditch and yet you're still yelling at me for riding in a car.

"The elders look the other way when the *youngie* drive. It's not fair that I'd be treated any differently." Samuel stormed toward the house, but stopped with his hand on the doorknob.

"We are different," Rebecca said, her voice quiet. "We are. We have to try harder."

Jake resisted the urge to reach out and touch Rebecca's arm in a gesture of comfort but he feared it wouldn't be accepted.

"What ever happened to forgiveness? Why can't they forgive and move on?" Samuel pounded his fist on the door.

Rebecca climbed a step and stopped. "I'm saddened that some people can't seem to forgive. It will take time."

"Were you dropped off without incident tonight?" Jake had to ask, bringing the conversation full circle. Last time he saw Samuel, he was hopping into a car with his friends.

"Yes, Uri dropped me off. He's a good driver, *mem*." Samuel took off his hat and scratched his head, leaving it in unkempt tufts.

"Uri was driving?"

"*Yah*, what does it matter?" Samuel crossed his arms over his chest, not waiting for an answer. "It doesn't help when you and the professor are asking questions and snooping around." His voice grew harsh. "I'll never be accepted by my friends. Professor Burke here accused us of selling drugs."

"You what? I…" Rebecca lifted a shaky hand to her lips.

Jake glanced at Rebecca. "We need to talk this through."

The look of distrust in her eyes tore at his heart. "But for now, I need you to trust me. Please go inside. Warm up."

Rebecca slowly nodded, the defeat evident on her face. Samuel turned to go with her, too, when Jake called out, "Hold up."

The young man slowly turned around but didn't say anything. Rebecca went inside and closed the door.

"Your mother is worried about you."

"I don't know why."

"You're an adult. I'm not sharing anything that you confided in me. So, if you need to talk…"

Jake's mind flashed to Samuel's friend Elmer, the young Amish man who had been in a lot of pain and had turned to drugs. Jake had pushed Elmer to go to his parents with his *issues*. A memory stabbed his gut. Maybe if Jake hadn't forced Elmer, the young man would still be walking God's green earth.

"I don't have anything to tell you." Samuel shuffled his feet and kept sneaking glances over his shoulder.

"If there's something going on, you can tell me. You're not alone. I can help you."

Samuel laughed, a harsh sound void of humor.

"You're just interested in your research. A good research paper. That's all we are to you. You don't really care."

Jake furrowed his brow. Was that what Samuel really thought? "I'm here if you need someone to talk to."

"Night, *Professor* Burke." Samuel disappeared inside.

Jake stood on the bottom step for a long moment. He turned toward the house when he heard the door handle click. Rebecca stood there, looking hesitant. "I'll ask Samuel to take you to your truck."

Jake shook his head slowly. "I'll be fine."

Rebecca nodded and closed the door. Jake strode down the drive to the road, to his truck parked down the way. He prayed the fresh air would clear his mind.

FIVE

Rebecca stood at the window and watched the professor until the darkness swallowed up his profile as he jogged toward his truck parked down the street. She hated to think what she would have done if he hadn't happened by. She probably would have had to claw her way out of the ditch.

Something niggled at her brain. *How was it that he had just come by?* She shook away her misgivings and stepped back from the window. The wet fabric of her skirt clung to her legs. *Yuck.*

She jogged up the stairs, stopping outside her son's bedroom. A thin line of light leaked from the bottom of his door. She lifted her hand to knock, then something inside her said to wait. A rational conversation wasn't going to be had while she shivered in her wet dress.

Samuel needed time to cool down, too.

Decision made, she retreated to her bedroom and changed into warm sleep clothes. After she brushed her teeth and washed her face, she climbed into her bed. Pulling the covers up, she said a quiet prayer for wisdom on how to reach her son. She couldn't bear to lose him. Not him, too.

Creak.

The house must be settling, Rebecca reasoned to herself. She rolled over and pulled the covers up over her shoulder. The nights were getting cooler. She took long breaths in and out but couldn't slow the thoughts racing through her head.

Harvest time was coming. She wondered how much longer she'd be able to manage the farm while she spent long hours at the diner.

The girls were spending more and more time with their aunt and uncle.

Everything that was important to her was slipping through her fingers.

Creak. Creak. Bang.

Rebecca froze and the sound of her shaky breath filled her ears. The noise had come from downstairs. She sprung up in bed and tossed the covers back in one swift motion. "Samuel!" she called. "Samuel, are you okay?"

When he didn't answer, a flush of dread heated her skin and made her dizzy. For once in her life, she wished she had a phone—one of the portable ones—to call for help.

She swung her legs out from under the covers and her toes hit the cool hardwood floor. She grabbed her robe from the hook and stuffed her arms into the sleeves. After hesitating at the bedroom door, she finally mustered the nerve to step into the dark hallway.

The house was quiet save for the ticking of a battery-powered clock downstairs in the kitchen, the sound traveling through the house.

Samuel's bedroom door yawned open revealing a dark space.

Her mouth went dry. "Samuel?"

Tick-tock-tick-tock mingled with her shaky breath.

Rebecca stepped into his room. Samuel's bed was empty. In the dark, she made out some of the shadows. The radio. The open laptop. The shock of seeing the forbidden items had worn off a bit, but still they taunted her. He had to get this worldliness out of his system. Come to realize that the Amish way of life was the only way.

Biting her lower lip, she left his room and descended the stairs. At that exact moment, the front door flew open and slammed against the wall. She couldn't make out his expression in the dark, but she knew it was her son. He pulled on something stuck in the wood of the door, then slammed the door shut.

She moved to the sitting room and turned on the kerosene lamp. Her growing unease swelled up, making her shudder. Rebecca tightened the tie on her robe around her waist. "Samuel, what is it? What's wrong?" Her gaze dropped to his hand. A silver blade glistened in the dim light. "What is that?" A lump of emotion clogged her throat.

Samuel glanced at the blade in his hand, as if he didn't know how it had gotten there. With a tight set of his mouth, he moved his other hand behind him. "You've got to leave things alone."

Rebecca took a step toward him, the wood creaking beneath her.

"Samuel," she pleaded, "please tell me what's going on. Did someone stick a knife in our front door?" A chill raced down her spine.

"Looks that way." His clipped words seemed forced. A cover for his own fear.

"Who would do such a thing? Did they leave a note under the blade?" Had she seen a piece of paper in his other hand?

The soft moonlight slanting through the window caught the naked fear in his eyes. He bowed his head, looking as if he wanted to say something.

"I want to help you," she pleaded. "Tell me."

He straightened. A hard expression darkened his eyes. "Stop asking questions. You're only making matters worse."

Rebecca hugged her arms around her middle. Suddenly, she felt sick. "What am I making worse?"

His stance widened and he pushed back his shoulders. Confident. Strong. Defiant. Her stomach twisted. So much like his father. "Isn't Rumspringa supposed to be a time of freedom for me? Time for me to explore on my own?"

"Is that what this is all about?" She shook her head. She couldn't believe it. "There has to be more to it. We're being harassed. Are people still angry about Willard?"

A muscle worked in his jaw, as if he couldn't find the words.

"Something else is going on. Tell me." She stepped forward and placed her hand gently on his arm, hoping to give him an opening. "Does it have to do with Elmer's death? I know you and he were good friends."

"You're worse than *Dat* in trying to control me."

Rebecca flattened her hands over her heart, feeling as if she had been stabbed. "I know you're hurting, but how could you compare me to your father? He was an evil man." The sting of tears burned the back of her eyes. "You need to apologize."

Samuel's lips thinned into a straight line. This was not the young man she'd raised. *Had Willard damaged him this much?*

A cold realization washed over her. She reached out to touch his arm and then thought better of it. "You are not your father's son. You are not Willard Fisher. You are Samuel. You are growing into a *gut* man." A million thoughts swirled in her brain. "Whatever is going on, I can help you. But you have to confide in me."

Samuel placed the knife on the table, crossed his arms and glared at her.

"If you can't confide in me, confide in Professor Burke."

"So he can tell you?" Samuel bit out the angry words.

"The professor hasn't told me anything. He said he didn't want to betray your trust." She angled her head, trying to get him to meet her eyes, but he seemed more interested in the dark ledge of the first stair. "Please, I want to help you."

Samuel rubbed his hand across his mussed hair. "Elmer lived in our barn after his father kicked him out for doing drugs."

Rebecca held her breath, waiting. "You should have told me. Perhaps I could have talked to his *dat* for him."

Samuel shook his head. "Mr. King was so angry. It wouldn't have mattered." The look of regret, sadness, guilt on her son's face hurt her deeply.

Rebecca softened her voice, longing to ease Samuel's guilt. "*Yah*, you were a *gut* friend. You did what you thought was right." It wasn't unheard of for people to take in their friends by providing a blanket and a soft spot to lay their head. Her son was no different.

Samuel ran a finger under his nose, then pointed upstairs. "All that stuff. The laptop. Everything. It was Elmer's. He asked me to hold it for him until he figured out what he was going to do next."

Relief and shame weighed heavy on her chest.

"You were a *gut* friend," she said again, determined to ease whatever was bothering him.

"No, I wasn't. I knew he was smoking weed the night he got into his car and drove away. It's all my fault."

Rebecca pointed to the knife with its sinister blade resting on the small table. "Is someone threatening you because of Elmer's death?"

"I—I think that's what this is about. Some of the guys have been harassing me. Telling me I should have stopped him from driving." He plowed his hand through his hair again. "But I left him in the barn and came inside. How was I to know he was going to get in the car?"

"You didn't." Rebecca wanted desperately to console him, but she knew he'd pull away. She was just happy he was finally opening up.

"Either way, I think you need to stop asking questions. It's only causing us more problems. People are also still mad about Willard. We have to let it go and then things will die down."

"We can't let people get away with harassing us. When will it stop?"

"Leave it alone, and it will stop." Samuel turned the key on the door, then picked up the knife and carried it into the kitchen. The metal blade clattered against the porcelain sink.

Was Samuel right? If she stopped asking questions, if she ignored the harassment, would whoever was doing this get bored and finally leave her family alone?

She closed her eyes and looked up at the night sky. Her wish was a foolish one.

Jake didn't have to teach his Intro to the Amish class until noon, so he drove out to the Fishers' farm early the next morning, hoping to catch the Yoder brothers and see what they'd been up to last night after they'd raced away from the Sunday singing in a car. He hoped the young Amish men he had gotten to know weren't involved in the horseplay that had gotten Rebecca thrown off her buggy.

A dark foreboding knotted his gut. What if it hadn't been horseplay and they had intentionally tried to hurt Rebecca?

Jake had called Sheriff Maxwell last night to ask if there had been any incidents, car accidents, things along that line, with the Amish last night. The sheriff claimed they hadn't had any calls. It had been a quiet night for the most part. The sheriff said he'd send additional patrols by the Fisher farm. Jake hoped that wouldn't cause more problems between Samuel and Rebecca.

Something about Samuel's evasive answers had kept Jake awake most of the night. The young man was either up to something or afraid of something. Or both. Jake had to get Samuel to trust him enough to open up. But he had to be careful not to alienate him like he had Elmer.

Jake parked on the dirt driveway. When he pushed open his car door, he heard angry voices coming from the barn. Jake couldn't make out the words, just the hostile tone. He broke into a jog and slowed at the doorway. Through the opening, he saw Samuel and Uri Yoder standing inches apart. Samuel had his arm up, ready to strike.

"Hey, hey, hey…" Jake yelled as he stormed into the barn. "What's going on?"

The two young men spun around to face him. Samuel lowered his fist and his shoulders sagged immediately. He crossed his arms and huffed, as if struggling to contain his anger.

"What's going on?" Jake repeated.

An aw-shucks smile spread across Uri's face. He took off his straw hat and rubbed the back of his hand across his forehead. "I mucked out the stalls yesterday and I was trying to get Samuel to take his turn."

Samuel's head snapped up, to call him a liar or perhaps surprised at the comment as if that wasn't what they had been arguing over.

Jake strolled in closer and dared put a hand on both men's shoulders. "What's really going on here?"

Samuel squirmed, stepping away from Jake's touch. "What Uri said. But since we're paying him to work here, he doesn't get to decide what *I* do." He hiked up his chin, daring Uri to defy him. "He and his brother are hired farm-hands. We tell them what to do."

Uri pulled away with a hard set of his jaw. He grabbed the pitchfork leaning against the stall. "Yeah, whatever. I thought we were friends."

"Wait up," Jake said to Uri. "Did you hear what happened last night?"

The two young men shared a quick glance that might have gone unnoticed if Jake hadn't been watching them closely.

"I told him this morning." Samuel glanced at the hay strewn on the barn floor and kicked it around with his boot.

"Is that the first you'd heard of it?" Jake watched Uri's expression carefully.

The young man's eyes narrowed into slits. "Are you accusing me of something? As if this day couldn't get any worse…" Without waiting for an answer, Uri stomped into the horse's stall and lifted a manure pile with the fork and dumped it into a nearby wheelbarrow.

Jake rubbed his jawline, realizing that antagonizing these young men wasn't going to help him and his research or, more important, Rebecca. She needed these young men to harvest the crops or she'd be in serious financial trouble.

Uri swiped his brow with the sleeve of his blue shirt. "I only learned of Mrs. Fisher's accident this morning." He lifted another load into the wheelbarrow.

Jake held his breath against the pungent smell.

"Are you both going to stand there and watch me? I have plenty of work to do and I don't appreciate an audience."

Determined to lighten the mood, Jake said, "You guys free to meet for dinner at the diner? Tonight maybe?"

Samuel lifted a shoulder, then let it drop. "Sure."

Uri set the pitchfork down and rested his elbow on the handle. "Food?" He smiled slyly. "I'm in."

Uri went back to work and Jake led Samuel toward the barn door. "Everything okay here, for real?"

Samuel rolled his eyes. "Yeah, everything's fine."

Jake nodded slowly. "Your *mem* home?"

"Inside making breakfast."

Jake didn't want to get all sentimental and scare the young man away, but he had to keep reminding Samuel that he was available if he needed anything.

Samuel's lips flattened into a thin line. He had reacted negatively when Jake first told him this. Perhaps the young man didn't want to be reminded that he didn't have a father. Even when he'd had one, the guy wasn't much of a role model.

The delicious scent of bacon filled the small space of Rebecca's kitchen. She lined the strips on a plate, careful not to let the grease splash.

Every muscle in her legs, arms and back ached from being thrown from the buggy last night. She was grateful the accident hadn't been worse than it had been, but she couldn't forget the angry exchange with Samuel in the middle of the night. Someone had stuck a blade in their front door.

Did it really have to do with Elmer's death? Something niggled at her. What more was Samuel hiding?

She wondered if it was time to call the sheriff, but she was caught between a rock and a hard place. Would Samuel be held responsible because he knew Elmer had been doing drugs before his death? Would Samuel shut down for good if she betrayed his confidence? She drew in a deep breath and let it out.

She couldn't think clearly. She had already lost so much. She tossed the tongs in the sink and glanced out the window. Her heart stuttered in her chest. Dressed in a handsome sport coat and clean shaven, the professor walked across the yard toward the house.

Instinctively, she smoothed what little hair wasn't hidden under her bonnet. She ran a hand down her skirt. When she reached the front door, he was already on the porch.

He tilted his head and a half smile slanted his lips.

Exactly what she didn't need.

"I didn't expect you this morning." She hoped her expression was inscrutable.

"How are you?"

Rebecca moved her arms as if to remind herself that her muscles did indeed still ache. "A little sore. But at least I'm in one piece…and dry." She ran a finger under her chin. "Were you in the barn?"

The professor nodded. "I paid a visit to Samuel and Uri. They seemed to be having a disagreement over chores."

"Hmm? That's unusual." Her mind went to Samuel's sour mood last night.

He took a step forward, the wood creaking under his weight. "What's on your mind?"

Rebecca worried her lower lip. "Someone stuck a knife in the door last night." She turned and ran her fingers over the small scar the knife had left.

Worry creased the corner of his eyes. "That's odd."

"I thought so, too." Rebecca nodded toward the inside. "Come in. I don't want Samuel to overhear."

They walked into the kitchen, and she encouraged the professor to sit while she started the coffee. The smell of freshly cooked bacon and eggs hung in the air.

"Samuel finally opened up to me and I need someone

objective to help me decide how to handle this." She had never expected to be a single parent.

She paused and pressed her lips into a thin line. "You have to promise me to keep this in confidence."

The professor gave her a quick nod.

"Samuel feels guilty because Elmer was living in our barn after his father kicked him out. He knew Elmer was on drugs the night he died."

"You had no idea Elmer was staying in your barn?"

"*Neh*. None. And Samuel claims all the electronics in his room belonged to Elmer."

"Did Samuel have an explanation for the knife in the door?"

"He thinks people are blaming him for Elmer's death with some residual anger about Willard. That if I stop asking questions, things will quietly go back to normal."

The professor got a faraway look in his eyes, as if he were processing all the information. "Samuel must think it's one of the *youngie* harassing you. Why else would he tell you to stop asking questions? Your questions led me to go to the Sunday singing."

A headache started behind her eyes. "What are they trying to hide?"

"Drug use? Or are they just angry and lashing out?"

She lifted a shaky hand to her collar, suddenly feeling very hot in her small kitchen. "I don't know. I don't know anything anymore."

"Do *you* think Samuel is into drugs?"

All the color drained from her already pale face. Isn't that why she had gone to the professor initially? To find out what was going on with Samuel, even if it included drugs.

"I don't know. I pray he isn't," she whispered.

The sound of footsteps on the back porch had Rebecca

swiping at unseen tears. Uri and Samuel burst through the back door.

"Breakfast is ready." She glanced at Uri and Samuel. "Where's Jonas?"

"He'll be in shortly," Uri said. He smiled at Rebecca, and washed his hands at the sink. "Everything looks great, Mrs. Fisher."

"Eat up. I know you boys have more work once you get home to your own farm."

The boys filled their plates and sat down.

"Working the land is *gut*. I feel close to *Gott*." Uri rubbed his hands together before picking up a piece of bacon and biting into it.

"Would you like to eat, Professor?"

He smiled at her and nodded. "Thank you." He filled a plate and took a seat at the head of the table. No one had sat in Willard's chair since he had left. The sensation that rolled over her was a strange one. She turned toward the counter and collected herself before joining everyone at the table.

They bowed their heads in silent prayer. A few minutes later, Jonas walked through the back door. "Sorry, my chores took a little bit longer this morning." He washed his hands, then sat to eat, too.

"Where are the little ones?" Jonas asked, curiosity in his eyes.

"They spent the night with their cousins."

"Oh."

The empty chairs at the table emphasized her daughters' absence. She missed her little girls. She hoped the day at the diner went quickly so she could pick up her daughters and bring them home. She felt out of sorts with her family scattered. She looked at Samuel who ate silently, a forlorn expression on his face.

And the one who was here seemed the farthest away.

SIX

"I was hoping I'd see you here." Hannah Spencer strolled into the diner midafternoon. She had a shopping bag in each hand.

"Nice to see you." Rebecca always felt a sense of loss when she saw her old friend. They were still friendly, but not like they had been while growing up. How could they be? Rebecca's husband had killed Hannah's sister and brother-in-law. No amount of time would allow either of them to forget that.

Hannah sat down at the counter and glanced around. "Place is quiet."

"Usually is around now. It's the lull between lunch and dinner." Rebecca grabbed a mug and poured a cup of coffee for her friend.

Hannah took a long sip. "Ahh…just how I like it."

Rebecca wiped the counter, mostly for something to do.

Flo grabbed a couple empty mugs from the other side of the counter and lifted them in greeting. "I'm going to take a short break before the dinner crowd starts rolling in." She turned and pushed open the door into the kitchen with her shoulder. As it swung back, the hinges creaked until the door finally stopped.

Hannah caught Rebecca's hand and squeezed it. "You

seem…tired, sad." She tilted her head. "Is there anything I can do to help?"

Rebecca glanced over her shoulder, trying to hide her emotions. Hannah was such a dear friend and she really missed her. Had missed her long before she'd left to marry Spencer. Hannah had run away from the Amish as a teenager only to return when her sister Ruth had been killed. By then, Willard had made it nearly impossible for Rebecca to have friends.

"I'll be okay." Rebecca fidgeted with the metal napkin holder, grabbing a stack of napkins from under the counter and refilling it.

Would she ever shake this guilt?

Rebecca looked at her friend, who was studying her. "How are things with you? Are you happy?" The question flew out of her mouth before she had a chance to call it back.

Hannah's brow creased. She tucked a strand of her neatly bobbed hair behind her ear and leaned forward. Probably a throwback to her Amish days, she didn't wear any makeup, yet she was one of the prettiest women Rebecca knew. Or maybe it was her personality Rebecca had always been drawn to.

"Yes, I'm very happy. I'd worried about the girls adjusting, but they seem to be doing well."

Rebecca ran her hand along the molded edge of the countertop. "Everyone has been through so much. I feel selfish for only thinking of my own problems." It wasn't the Amish way. The Amish considered community and not individuality.

Rebecca noticed a puddle of water on the counter, so she picked up the dishtowel and wiped it up. Then, twisting the towel in her hands, she said, "Maybe I should leave Apple Creek. Take the girls—Samuel if he'll go—and make a fresh start in another Amish community." She stared off into the middle distance, not really aware of her surroundings. "I could move closer to Rochester. There are a few Amish church districts that are in fellowship with Apple Creek."

Hannah reached out and clutched her friend's hand. "Oh, you can't run away. We'd miss you too much. Apple Creek is your home."

Hannah's voice grew soft. "This *is* your home."

Rebecca's friend's face grew blurry. "It doesn't feel like home anymore."

Jake smiled as Rebecca approached their table that evening. She handed a menu to him and Samuel. "Are you expecting anyone else?" she asked, all business.

"Yes." Jake held up three fingers. "Three more."

She set three extra plastic menus at the edge of the table. "I'll be right back with the silverware and water."

"Thank you," both men said in unison.

Rebecca turned and walked away.

Resting his forearms on the edge of the table, Jake leaned toward Samuel and lowered his voice. "You have no reason to feel guilty over Elmer's death."

Samuel's mouth fell open, then his posture sagged. "Of course my *mem* told you everything."

"She's worried about you."

The young man rolled his eyes.

Jake tapped his fingers on the table, trying to figure out how to broach the subject. *Be direct.*

"If anyone should feel guilty, it's me."

Samuel slowly met Jake's gaze but didn't say anything.

"During one of our meetings, I sensed Elmer was high. I confronted him. At first Elmer denied it, but then he finally told me he was just—" Jake lifted his hands to use air quotes "—smoking a little pot. No biggie."

Jake ran a hand across his face, then glanced over his shoulder to make sure Rebecca wasn't coming. "I forced him to tell his father."

Samuel tucked his chin closer to his chest and a deep line furrowed his brow in disbelief. "Why would you do that?"

"I watched my own father die from addiction. Alcohol." Jake slowly shook his head, reliving every misstep he had taken with Elmer. "I thought I was doing the right thing." He shrugged, hoping the nonchalant gesture would ease the weight bearing down on his chest. "But as you know, his father kicked him out. He spiraled downward from there." He studied the palm of his hand, unable to look into Samuel's eyes. "If anyone's to blame, it's me."

Samuel let out a long breath.

Jake finally lifted his head and pinned the young man across from him with his gaze. "I want you to know that if you need someone to talk to I'm here. Guilt is an unrelenting companion."

The young man snorted. "You'll tell my *mem*."

Jake shook his head. "Not if you don't want me to." He set his clasped hands in front of him on the table. "If you're caught up in drugs, I want to help you."

"Wait a minute—" Samuel stopped whatever he was about to say. Jake glanced over his shoulder and saw Rebecca returning with a tray of glasses filled with ice water.

Just then the door opened and Tommy, Jake's teaching assistant, strolled into the diner and slipped into the seat next to Samuel.

Rebecca smiled. "I'll give you a few minutes to read the menu." Jake suspected that no one who frequented the Apple Creek Diner actually needed to consult the menu.

A muscle ticked in Samuel's jaw and Jake regretted that they hadn't had a couple more minutes to talk in private.

Fidgeting in his seat as if he had somewhere else to go, Tommy drummed his fingers on the plastic menu. "Uri called me a few minutes ago. He and Jonas can't make it. They had some chores at home."

"Maybe we should meet another time." Samuel suddenly seemed agitated, glancing over his shoulder at the window.

Jake smiled. "You need to eat anyway, right? We'll meet again when the Yoder brothers are free."

Samuel slumped back in the booth and crossed his arms over his chest. "Yeah, I guess."

Rebecca approached the table, holding a pen and pad in her hands. "Ready to order or are you still waiting for more guests?"

"Change of plans. It'll be just us."

The three men placed their orders. Rebecca caught Jake's eye and he smiled. "Thank you."

Her pale cheeks flushed before she turned to put the orders in.

Jake took a sip of his water and watched Samuel over the rim of his glass. He wondered if they'd ever get to finish that conversation. Had Samuel been about to open up to him?

At a nearby table, a college student waved his hand eagerly, trying to get Rebecca's attention. "Um, we'd like to order, like, sometime this week."

"I hate that my *mem* has to work here," Samuel said. "She shouldn't have to. My father ruined everything."

"You have to forgive him. Move on," Jake suggested.

Samuel furrowed his brows. "Maybe it's time I jumped the fence," he said, using the term the Amish had for leaving the community. The distant look in his brown eyes suggested he was already envisioning it.

Jake watched Rebecca lift a hold-on-a-minute finger to the college student before tacking their order onto the silver wheel above the window leading into the kitchen of the old-fashioned diner. She then refilled the coffee mug of a gentleman sitting at the counter. She smiled and made small talk with the man before making her way over to the table of college students.

Jake smiled inwardly. She'd handled the rude customer with quiet aplomb.

He turned his attention back to Samuel. "Your *mem* would be devastated if you left." Jake hated to heap guilt on this young man, but he needed to know. "Make sure your decisions are for the right reasons. Give it some time. You're still grieving over your friend."

"Leaving isn't always the best answer." Tommy tore off the wrapper to the straw, leaving the tip in place. "I mean," he said, then blew the last bit of paper off his straw, "the grass ain't always greener on the other side. I've had to work my butt off to make money to pay for college."

Jake was ready to quip that he didn't work Tommy *that* hard but decided to let it go. He wanted to hear what Tommy had to say as someone who had walked away from the Amish way of life.

Tommy took a sip of his water through the straw, watching Samuel carefully. "You have an eighth-grade education. What kind of job do you think you're going to get—" he gestured with his chin toward the window "—out there? Do you know how hard it is to get a job? A good paying job?" He stabbed the ice with the straw. The ice clattered against the glass. "Even if you get a job, do you think you can support yourself and a family?" He laughed and shook his head.

"I can work with my hands," Samuel said. "There are several successful Amish businesses in town."

"But you won't be Amish anymore," Tommy said, twisting his lips. "Once you leave small-town Apple Creek, you'd be surprised at how many businesses require a four-year degree to allow you to work with your hands."

Samuel groaned.

This was exactly the complaint Jake's father had had after leaving the Amish. He hadn't been able to get a decent job and what little money he had managed to make he spent on liquor.

"It was a lot of work for me to get my GED and then get into college. Do you think college is cheap?" Tommy shook his head dramatically. "Nope, now I gotta pay for college. Sure, I'll be done in June, but it's been a long road. Now I got loans to pay back. Don't go thinking running away from home is going to solve your problems."

Silence settled over the table. Jake was surprised to hear his assistant talk this bluntly. Normally, Tommy talked fondly about his experiences as an *Englisher*. How he was happy to escape the mind-numbing tedium of life on a farm.

To each his own, Jake supposed. Letting Samuel know the stark reality of leaving was a good idea.

Rebecca returned with their food and left just as quickly. Perhaps she was hoping her son was confiding in Jake so he could help him.

"How long have you been gone?" Samuel asked Tommy, genuine curiosity in his tone.

Tommy squirted ketchup onto his plate, picked up a French fry and swirled it in the red blob. "I left when I was eighteen. Had to work a bunch of meaningless jobs to pay the rent, buy food…" He took a bite out of his French fry "I studied for two years to get my high school GED. Another year to get accepted to Genwego State University. Now I'm a senior." He exhaled. "It's been a long road."

"If *you* can do it, I can…" Samuel started. The desperation in his voice caught Jake off guard.

Tommy lifted his eyes to Rebecca, who was hustling from table to table in the busy dining room. "Like Professor Burke said, your *mem* would be devastated. Why don't you lay low for a while? *Really* think about it. Like I said, the grass isn't always greener."

Samuel slouched into the booth again, seemingly agitated. "I need to get away. To protect my *mem*. My little sisters." He lifted his backside off the bench and handed a wadded piece of paper to Jake. "Last night, someone stuck a knife into the front door."

"Your *mem* told me," Jake said.

Samuel nodded, as if this didn't surprise him.

"This was left under the knife. I didn't show her."

Jake met the young man's gaze, then smoothed out the piece of paper.

Keep your mouth shut.

Samuel bit his lower lip, struggling to contain his emotions.

"Are they referring to you or your mother?"

"I…I think me," Samuel said. "I believe it was one of the Yoder brothers."

Jake tugged on the collar of his shirt. "Is that why you were fighting this morning in the barn?"

Samuel nodded. "Uri denied he left the note. Told me I was crazy."

Tommy's expression remained placid.

"Why would the Yoder brothers want you to keep your mouth shut?" Jake watched Samuel carefully.

"They're…" Samuel's voice wavered as if he was having second thoughts. "…They're growing marijuana on our farm."

A loud crash made Jake spin around.

Rebecca's scalp tingled as she stared down at the white shards of what had once been ceramic plates, mingled with French fries, buns and hamburger patties.

She bent over and scrambled to pick up the mess, her thoughts all jumbled. "I'm sorry. So, sorry," she muttered to the patrons at the booth next to her son's. The voices and sounds of the diner swirled around her, growing more distant and fuzzy. Blinking did nothing to tamp down the dizziness.

She glanced toward the kitchen, waiting for her boss to storm out in full rant mode. She had never dropped a platter of dishes before.

Had she misheard? Uri and Jonas were growing marijuana on her farm?

The few French fries she had snacked on earlier revolted in her stomach.

A solid hand cupped her elbow. Rebecca looked up into the professor's warm brown eyes. "Come on." He eased her to a standing position. "Come over here. Sit down."

"I can't. I have to clean up this mess." She stared at the broken plate in one hand and the leaf of lettuce in the other. A throbbing pain started behind her eyes.

The professor took the piece of ceramic out of her hand. "It can wait." He guided her to the seat he had vacated. She dropped the lettuce on a napkin and lifted her gaze to her son.

Rebecca threaded her fingers, leaned forward and whispered. "What did you say?" She fought the hysteria welling up inside her, unwilling to make more of a spectacle of herself. She was tired of being a spectacle.

Samuel leaned across the table, desperation in his voice. "Uri and Jonas are growing marijuana plants on our land." He lowered his head and furtively glanced around the diner.

Rebecca did the same. Several diners were staring at their table. A busboy was cleaning up the mess she had made. Rebecca leaned past the professor and touched the young man's shoulder. "Thank you, Jason. I was clumsy."

The young man smiled. "No problem, Mrs. Fisher. I got it." He put the last remnant of the ruined dinner in a large gray bus tub. "I'll sweep up the rest."

Rebecca looked up, confusion swirling around her head. "Oh, I need to apologize to the table for dropping their food. I need—"

He touched her hand. "Hold on."

She stared at him, but couldn't really see him. Her mind was reeling.

Flo strolled over and smiled. "I'll take care of the table. Don't worry."

Tears stung the back of Rebecca's nose. "Thank you."

As the other diners seemed to go back to their meals and the din in the diner returned to its normal level, Rebecca kept her voice low, confident no one would overhear her. "Why did you let them?" she asked Samuel.

Hurt lingered in her son's eyes. "I didn't. I only figured out what they were doing a few months ago. Shortly before Elmer's accident." He bowed his head, then looked back up. "That's why I felt bad about Elmer. It wasn't simply because I knew he was doing drugs. It was because I didn't stop Uri and Jonas for providing him with drugs."

All the color seemed to have drained out of Samuel's face. "I'm sorry I wasn't completely honest with you, *Mem*."

"How did you figure out they were growing marijuana?" Tommy spoke for the first time.

"Elmer was living in our barn and he asked me for drugs."

Rebecca pressed her fingers into her temples.

"I had no idea what he was talking about. Elmer told me the plants weren't ready yet, but Uri had some drugs on him to sell," Samuel continued. "I don't know where he got them. Maybe they used someone else's land before ours."

"I don't understand any of this."

"I should have told someone. Maybe Elmer wouldn't have died."

"And you saw the plants?" Tommy asked.

Samuel scrubbed a hand across his face and frowned. "Elmer showed me. He led me through the cornfields. In the far back corner of the field, I found them. There were these plants, plants like I had never seen."

"How did you know what they were?" Tommy asked, pushing his empty plate to the center of the table.

Samuel's cheeks flushed. "I took a picture of them with my phone and then did a Google search."

Rebecca ran a hand across her forehead. She had no idea what he was talking about. Her mouth grew dry. "Why didn't you tell me?"

"They told me they wouldn't do it again. I had to keep quiet through harvest season.

"Then, a few days later Elmer died. They warned me if I told anyone about the marijuana, people would blame me for Elmer's death. That law enforcement would take away our land."

"Did they threaten you to keep you quiet?" the professor asked.

"They bribed me by giving me things." Deep lines marred his forehead. "Like the laptop. My cell phone."

He averted his gaze. "They weren't Elmer's things. I wasn't truthful last night, *Mem*. I just wanted all this to stop."

Rebecca's pulse beat loudly in her ears.

"I should have told you, but I got caught up in the lies and I was afraid. I'm sorry." He pushed his hand through his hair, leaving it standing up, reminding Rebecca of the little boy who used to come downstairs in his night clothes asking for apple biscuits. What she wouldn't do to go back to those days.

"But my conscience started to bother me. I thought I'd be no better than my…than Willard. I didn't want to get Jonas and Uri in trouble. I told them they had to destroy the crops. Get them off our property."

"How did they respond?" Tommy asked, pulling his cell phone out and checking the screen.

Samuel bowed his head. "They threatened *Mem* if I didn't allow the plants to come to harvest. When you started asking around, they started scaring you. I fear they ran you off the road last night, but I promise you, I wasn't in the car."

How could these boys she'd welcomed into her home try to hurt her?

Rebecca closed her eyes briefly. Fear and confusion gave way to a strange sense of relief. "You did the right thing. Now I can go to Mr. and Mrs. Yoder. They're good people. They'll get their sons to listen. Get them to obey."

Samuel looked up, an air of disbelief in his expression. "That's not going to work."

"We have to do something," Rebecca said in a soft voice.

"We should call the sheriff," the professor said.

Rebecca shook her head adamantly. "*Neh*. We can't call the sheriff. I don't want to get the boys in trouble with law enforcement. It's not the Amish way."

"What they did is illegal," the professor said.

"We need to approach their parents first. Mr. Yoder will rein his sons in. I know it."

The professor stared at her for a minute before nodding. "We'll start with the parents, but I can't promise you we won't call the sheriff."

SEVEN

Jake climbed into his truck and looked in the rearview mirror. He could see Samuel in the backseat of the extended cab, staring out the window, an unreadable expression on his face.

"It's going to be okay, Samuel." Rebecca buckled her seat belt and slumped into the seat next to Jake. The smell of French fries clung to her clothes. "You did the right thing by telling us. Everything is going to be okay." Her statement sounded more like a question, suggesting she had no idea if everything was going to be okay. If only Jake could give her assurances.

Rebecca turned to Jake. "Thanks for the ride. It saves me paying the hired driver. Are you sure it's not too much trouble to pick up my daughters after we speak to Mr. Yoder?"

"No trouble at all."

When Tommy came out of the diner after paying the bill with Jake's credit card, Jake lowered the driver's side window. Tommy handed the card to him and said, "I'm going to bum a ride from one of my friends back to the university." Tommy leaned in and smiled weakly at Samuel in the backseat. He lowered his voice. "I'd rather not get caught up in all this… I think if I keep some distance, we won't jeopardize my association with the Amish."

"Have a good night, then." Jake watched Tommy, dressed in jeans and a university sweatshirt, stroll away. Jake had a hard time imagining Tommy growing up Amish. He had a worldly way about him.

Jake rolled up the window and pulled out onto Main Street. The silence in the truck was like a fourth occupant who couldn't be ignored.

When his truck crested the country road, Jake glanced in the rearview mirror and studied an unsuspecting Samuel. The young Amish man took off his hat and scrubbed a hand over his hair. The lines around his eyes revealed his stress.

"I'm not sure I'm ready to talk to the Yoders. Are we doing the right thing?" Rebecca asked in a soft voice laced with concern and worry.

Jake wanted to reassure her, tell her everything was going to be fine, but he knew they had a rough road ahead of them. "It's a start, but I'd feel better if we had called the sheriff."

"Not yet. Let's keep this matter among the Amish." She gave Jake a pointed glare. Jake, who was clearly not Amish.

Samuel made a disagreeable noise. "What have I done?" he muttered. "I should have kept quiet."

"You couldn't keep going on this way. You haven't been yourself. You've done the right thing. We'll help you straighten out this mess. *Without* the sheriff," Rebecca added for emphasis.

Jake parked in front of the Yoders' farm. "You can wait here." Jake felt strangely protective of Rebecca.

"No, I need to talk to the Yoders myself. I've known them for a long time. They've known my family."

Samuel didn't say anything as he climbed out of the truck.

A soft light glowed in the front window. Jake smiled at Samuel, trying to reassure him.

Jake knocked, and a few seconds later an older gentleman opened the door. "*Yah?* How can I help you?" The line between his eyes eased when he noticed Rebecca. "Rebecca, is something wrong?"

"Are Uri and Jonas home?" she asked, a hint of apology in her tone.

Mr. Yoder fingered his unkempt beard. "*Yah*, we're finishing our meal." He turned away from the door without inviting them in. From inside, Jake heard a lot of commotion, perhaps standard when a family had ten children.

Jake's stomach pitched. It had been a little over three months ago when he pushed Elmer to go to his father regarding his drug use. Jake never could have imagined the series of events that would follow, ending in tragedy. And here he was, an outsider standing on his Amish neighbor's stoop.

Uri appeared at the door with an innocent-looking expression. "What's going on?"

"Where's your brother?"

Uri grabbed the door and opened it wider. Jonas stood next to his father. His expression was less cocky than his brother's.

"What's going on?" Mr. Yoder asked with a strong Pennsylvania Dutch accent.

"We believe your sons have been growing marijuana on Rebecca's farm."

Mr. Yoder pulled his head back. A look of confusion and fear crossed his dark eyes. "Growing what?"

"Marijuana," Samuel spoke up for the first time. "They plan on selling it and making a lot of money."

A muscle ticked in Uri's jaw and Jonas gave his brother a sideways glance.

Mr. Yoder turned to face his sons. "Is this true?" Without waiting for an answer, he turned back to Rebecca. "Who told you my sons planted this marijuana?"

"*My* son." Rebecca played with the folds of her gown.

"*Dat*, me and Jonas had nothing to do with those crops."

"You knew about the marijuana?" his father asked accusingly.

"I didn't know what it was until Samuel told me."

"That's not true," Samuel bit out. "That's not true at all."

Uri turned to his father, a dark look in his eyes. "*Dat*, I have never lied to you. I was afraid to say anything for fear we'd be fired. Jonas and I know how much this family needs the extra money from our work as farmhands."

Mr. Yoder flinched.

Uri bowed his head contritely. "Who are you going to believe? Me or Samuel, *Willard Fisher's* son?"

Rebecca stumbled backward and Jake grabbed her arm to steady her. "Keep calm," he whispered close to her ear.

Mr. Yoder ran his hand down his beard again. "The crops are on *your farm*, Rebecca. Don't come here and accuse my boys of these things. They are *gut* boys." Mr. Yoder hiked his chin. "I think it's time you left."

Mr. Yoder stepped out onto the porch and pulled the door closed behind him, leaving his sons inside.

"My son isn't lying," Rebecca said. "Your sons have taken advantage of my situation and used my land to grow marijuana."

Mr. Yoder pinched his lips together and shook his head. "I suggest you leave before I call the sheriff."

Jake squeezed Rebecca's elbow. "Let's go."

She yanked her elbow away. "Mr. Yoder," she pleaded.

Mr. Yoder stood his ground. "Sounds like a convenient

excuse. How do you know Samuel's not looking for a way out?" The anger flashed in the older man's eyes.

"*Mem*, I had nothing to do with those crops."

"I suggest you get your son under control." Mr. Yoder paused a long few seconds. "My sons won't be working on your farm any longer. It seems your family is a bad influence." And with that, he shut the door on the conversation.

With a firm hand to the small of her back, Jake led Rebecca to his truck. When Samuel didn't follow, Jake called to him over his shoulder. *"Let's go."* Jake didn't want any more trouble tonight that would require either him or the Yoders to call the sheriff. "We have to pick up your sisters."

Right now it was their word against Samuel's, and after recent events, the sheriff might be more likely to believe the Yoders.

That night in bed, Rebecca tossed and turned, a million things going through her mind. What if Samuel was lying? What if he had been looking for a way out and decided to pin his mistake on the Yoders? What if he was growing the marijuana?

Willard had committed murder under her watch and she'd had no idea.

Rebecca rolled over and punched her pillow. She felt sick.

After everything Willard had done to put her family in a bad light, how could she and Samuel convince anyone he was telling the truth? *If* he was telling the truth. Her family wasn't exactly well respected in the Amish community.

Feeling queasy, Rebecca propped up her pillows, hoping that would help. She took a deep breath.

Nothing would help.

Rebecca had hoped Samuel would confide in her once

she put her daughters to bed, but he had retreated to his room and slammed the door.

Nothing—yet everything—had changed.

A tear slid down her cheek and plopped on the pillow. She felt as if her relationship with Samuel was beyond repair.

Could she ever reach him now?

Closing her eyes, she tried to relax and think of her blessings: Katie and Grace. Rebecca wanted to hold everyone she loved close. As if that could stop her world from spinning out of control.

The fierce protectiveness she felt for her family was also reminiscent of the days after Willard's arrest. Yet, after her husband had been arrested, Rebecca also had felt a strange sense of freedom, unlike she'd ever had.

Had this freedom ruined Samuel?

Rebecca pulled her quilt up to her chin and smoothed the fabric, running her fingers along the careful stitching she and her mother had done back when Rebecca still had dreams of a happy marriage and a quiet life in Apple Creek.

Her life had turned out nothing like she had planned.

No one planned to marry a murderer.

Rebecca closed her eyes. Sweet, handsome Jake filled her mind. *The professor.* She didn't know if she'd ever be able to call him anything else. She felt that she'd be breaching the social norms if she called him Jake.

Jake. Jacob.

Nervousness tingled across her skin. The professor had told her he'd be back tomorrow between the classes he taught at the university. They could plan their next steps then. He promised he wouldn't call the sheriff, and she only prayed the Yoders didn't either. It was unlikely; the Amish preferred to handle things on their own.

A new surge of adrenaline made her restless. Rebecca tossed back the covers and swung her legs over the edge. She hated that she doubted her son. She closed her eyes and prayed for God's guidance. And for help in believing in a young man she had grown to consider her son.

Maybe her influence had come too late.

Pacing the hardwood floor, she suddenly had the urge to do something. She could no longer lead a passive life waiting for her world to implode. Waiting for someone to help her. She had to help herself.

Help her family.

She pulled back the curtain on the window. A bright moon and a million stars dotted the night sky. Besides the barn and a few outbuildings, all she could see were the crops. Acres and acres of corn.

And marijuana.

Dressed in her nightclothes, she slipped into her young daughters' bedroom and kissed each of them on the forehead, breathing in their fresh scent. Her daughters consistently brought her joy and she'd do whatever it took to protect them from further hurt.

She passed Samuel's closed door, lingering long enough to drag her fingers along the cool wood.

Oh, Samuel, I wish you'd come to me a long time ago. Now I don't know what to believe...

The wood on the stairs creaked under her weight as she descended to the first floor, her hand gliding along the smooth banister, the one her children's great-grandfather had carved. The rock solidness of her life, the one built on the foundation of her family's Amish ancestors, was crumbling around her.

Rebecca yanked her coat from the hook by the back door, slipped her bare feet into her cold boots and stepped out onto the back porch. The fall air smelled crisp. Fresh. Refreshing.

She'd never be happy anywhere but here. On a farm. Close to God's creation. The moonlight glowed brightly in the night sky, casting the crops in a white glow.

Before she lost her nerve, she strode to the barn. She pulled back the heavy door and stepped inside, slivers of moonlight glinting in between the wood slats. Buttercup neighed at her intrusion before settling back in.

Crossing to the back of the barn where Willard had kept his tools, she grabbed a sickle from its hook. She wondered if there was a better tool, but decided this would have to do. Growing up on a farm, she wasn't unfamiliar with the tools, she just wasn't as experienced with using them as her older brothers had been.

Gripping the wood handle tightly in her right hand, she trudged toward the cornfields. Based on Samuel's description, the evil drugs should be hidden in the far corner of the field where her property ended and a thick lot of trees started.

Holding the sickle by her side, she held her left hand out to push aside the stalks as she strode deeper into the fields. The earth shifted under her footsteps, adding to her sense of unsteadiness. Somewhere in the distance, she heard the *hoot-hoot-hoot* of an owl.

Goose bumps raced across her flesh. She slowed her pace and turned around, unsure if the sounds she heard were of her own making or if they were out of place.

A giggle bubbled up. *Out of place?* There was nothing about this entire scene that made sense. Nerves implored her to go back home. Crawl into bed and cover her head. To never get out of bed again.

"No, I'm going to do this," she muttered. "I'm going to protect my family."

Tightening her grip on the sickle, she turned and walked forward. Her sense of hopelessness had been replaced by something else. Confidence. Assuredness. Determination.

She could do something. Help Samuel.

Just as Samuel had said, tall bushy plants grew where the corn stopped. *This must be the marijuana.* Feeling their soft leaves, a hint of citrus tickled her nose. How dare the Yoder boys betray her trust and use her land to grow drugs.

The tired, weary face of Mrs. King slammed into her memory. Poor Elmer had been high on drugs when he'd crashed his car into a tree.

Rebecca feared she was going to be sick. She focused all her attention on calming breaths until her stomach settled.

A new emotion, one she hadn't allowed herself to feel when Willard was arrested, washed over her. *Rage.*

She lifted the solid sickle and whacked at the thick stem of the unfamiliar plants. The sharp blade sliced through the stem, felling the plant. She lifted her hand again and again. *Thwack. Thwack. Thwack.*

The plants rustled as they fell.

The muscles in her shoulders and arms began to ache. Tears streaming down her cheeks, she tossed the sickle aside. Hands planted on her hips, she studied her destruction. She had barely made a dent in the illegal crops.

Rebecca pressed her lips together and lifted her eyes. The first hint of a new dawn touched the sky. She rolled her shoulders back, trying to ease the tension.

A strangled cry sounded behind her. Slowly she turned and a dark figure advanced on her.

"Samuel?"

A scream got trapped in her throat. The figure lifted his hand.

Rebecca lifted her arms to defend against the blow. She was no match.

The pain on the top of her head was the last thing she remembered as her knees buckled and the earth rushed up to meet her.

Jake jumped into his truck as soon as he had gotten the phone call from Samuel. Rebecca's son had woken up to his little sisters' tears because they couldn't find their mother.

Jake exceeded the speed limit, the engine in his old truck straining to keep pace. He offered a prayer, the first he could remember since childhood, that Rebecca was safe. Perhaps Samuel had been lax in his search for his mother and she was safe. The knot twisted in his gut. Or had someone retaliated against her because of her inquiries?

He shook his head. He couldn't think the worst.

Once he arrived at Rebecca's home, he ran up to the porch. Samuel opened the door before Jake had a chance to knock.

"Has your mom returned?"

Samuel had his hand on Grace's shoulder. Katie hung back, her face stained with tears.

"No. I checked the barn, but I didn't want to leave my sisters for too long. It's unlike *Mem* to leave the girls without asking me to watch them. They're only six and eight."

Jake turned and gazed out over the land. Sun peaked over the horizon. The promise of a beautiful new day was at odds with this horrible sense of foreboding.

Really, she could be anywhere: the barn, the fields, or maybe she *had* gone out. But a tiny whisper in his brain grew louder by the second. *Something's happened to Rebecca!*

Jake clamped his jaw, not wanting to alarm the young girls. "When was the last time you saw your mother?"

After they all came to the consensus that they hadn't seen their mother since they had gone to bed last night,

Jake told Samuel to stay inside the house with his little sisters while he went outside to look for her.

"Maybe you missed her when you checked the barn earlier. Could she be milking a cow?"

Katie, the older of the two girls, tilted her head and scrunched up her nose. "We don't have a cow. *Mem* brings milk home from the market now. It's easier. We have an icebox."

"Well, maybe she's checking on Buttercup."

The younger of the two took a step forward, eager for an adventure. "Let me come with you. I like to give Buttercup carrots."

Jake reached out and touched the top of the young girl's soft hair and smiled. "Later, okay."

Grace pouted and spun on her heels, her loose curls flying out behind her.

"Stay here." Jake locked gazes with Samuel. "I'll be right back."

Jake jogged down the steps and toward the barn, calling Rebecca's name. Disquiet crept into his bones and he worried he hadn't done enough to keep Rebecca safe. He also began to wonder how he had allowed himself to become so involved with his Amish neighbors when his intent had been to learn about them, not become entangled in their lives.

He supposed his mission was irrevocably intertwined.

Jake wiped a bead of sweat trickling down his forehead.

Where would she have gone?

"I'm sick of doing nothing." Rebecca's words from last night pinged around his brain. "I'm tired of feeling hopeless. Of not being able to keep my family together."

Jake knew she wouldn't hurt herself, but the worry kept resurfacing. He thought of his own father, who drank himself to death after Jake's mother died. Some people couldn't see past their own grief.

Scrubbing a hand across his face, he had an inkling she might have gone in search of the marijuana crops. He jogged toward the cornstalks. To the far corner of the lot. To where Samuel had claimed the Yoder brothers had planted the marijuana.

Something was drawing him there.

Still calling her name, Jake ran through the stalks, the smell of earth and dried corn filling his nose. Then, suddenly the corn ended and a different kind of plant started.

A rock solidified in his gut. It looked as if someone had been hacking away at the plants.

"Rebecca?" he called again, the frantic whoosh of his pulse drowning out any possible answer.

Jake took a few more cautious steps.

"God, help me find her," he finally muttered, the words feeling foreign on his lips. "Rebecca, where are you?"

As Jake pushed through the plants, he heard a soft moan.

He stopped, his heart pounding against his chest. "Rebecca?"

He strained to hear. The moan came again. He spun around and ran to the pile of felled marijuana plants. He found Rebecca lying there, her face covered in blood.

In a frenzy, he tossed aside the plants and knelt down beside a battered and bloodied Rebecca.

Gingerly, he swept her hair out of her eyes, tugging it away from the dried blood. "Can you hear me?"

Her eyes fluttered but didn't open. *She's not dead. There's hope. Thank you, God.*

Jake reached down and grabbed her hand and squeezed.

"I'm here. You're going to be okay." With his other hand, he reached into his back pocket. "I'm going to call an ambulance."

EIGHT

A persistent tugging near Rebecca's forehead nudged her out of the blackness. She focused all her energy on opening her eyes, but they wouldn't budge. A strong citrusy-grass smell clogged her nose.

Why can't I open my eyes?

She craned her neck and a horrible pain sliced through her head. She tried to lift her hand to touch it, but her limbs didn't want to cooperate.

A familiar soothing voice threaded into her subconscious. *I'm here... You're going to be okay...*

She finally pried her eyes open a sliver and the line of light made her brain explode. Instinctively, she snapped her eyes shut again and groaned.

A warm hand squeezed hers. "Take it easy. Don't try to move. I've called for an ambulance."

Dread squirmed its way in to keep her fear and queasiness company.

Rebecca's mouth grew dry. *"Neh..."*

"Don't try to talk."

She shook her head slowly and immediately realized her mistake. She pressed her lips together against the nausea.

"No ambulance," she finally whispered, her voice raspy. "No police."

The professor dragged his warm thumb gently across her cheek. The small gesture provided comfort. She couldn't remember what happened. One minute she was hacking away at the marijuana plants and then...

Closing her eyes, flashes of memory assaulted her. Standing in the field admiring the first hint of early morning sky. Turning around. A dark shadow.

Samuel?

Her stomach revolted at the thought of her own son striking her.

Neh, neh. Rebecca refused to believe that.

She covered her mouth, as if she feared his name might slip past her lips.

"What is it?" the professor said in a soothing voice. "Do you know who did this to you?"

"*Neh.* Please..." She tried to sit up again and he touched her shoulder.

"You have to wait for the ambulance. It's not safe to move since I don't know if anything's broken."

"Don't you understand?" Her voice came out raspy. "You can't call an ambulance...the sheriff will come. The plants."

"Your well-being is more important," the professor said.

"Help me get to the house so the sheriff won't see what's back here." Her brain hurt with the effort of every word.

Kneeling over her, the professor shook his head. "I can't do that."

"Why not?" Anger and nausea competed for her attention.

"I can't risk it. I don't know where you're hurt."

Rebecca struggled to move into a seated position, and the professor seemed to capitulate by offering her a hand, steadying her. "Don't try to stand."

Adrenaline surged in her veins. "Are the girls okay?

Samuel?" She tried to push off the ground, but the palm of her hand sank into the earth. "I have to check on my family."

The professor touched her arm in a soothing gesture. "Everyone is okay. Samuel's in the house with the girls. I told them to stay put."

Rebecca lifted her arm to touch her forehead, and the effort made her groan.

"Did you see who attacked you?"

Rebecca caught herself before she shook her poor head. *"Neh."*

"What were you doing out here?"

She squinted up at the professor, trying to minimize the amount of light hitting her brain. "Destroying these crops." She clawed at one of the discarded plants next to her.

"In the middle of the night?" The protectiveness in his voice made her feel like she hadn't felt in a long time.

Too bad the professor was an *Englisher*.

In the distance she heard a siren, and panic raced through her. "You have to tell the children I'm okay. They'll worry when they see the ambulance."

The professor squeezed her hand and smiled. "Are you sure?"

"Please," she begged. "You need to warn them so they don't worry."

Rebecca watched as the professor ran through the cornstalks. Desperate to get away from the marijuana crops, Rebecca struggled to her feet. The world tilted and her empty stomach heaved.

With one hand to her forehead and the other to her belly, she moved one foot in front of the other through the tall cornstalks.

Please help me, Lord.

The sound of the sirens grew closer, adding to the clanging in her head. She paused and leaned over, bracing her hands on her knees. It didn't help.

Dizzy, she straightened and walked shakily forward. Finally, she stepped onto the hard-packed surface of her driveway. The lights on the ambulance caught her eye before her gaze landed on the professor coming out of the house.

Tiny stars danced in her line of vision before darkness consumed her and she collapsed.

With a bouquet of wildflowers in his hand, Jake lingered in the doorway of Rebecca's hospital room while she slept. Her shiny brown hair, usually wound in a bun and hidden under a bonnet, was splayed on the white pillow. A white bandage covered a portion of her forehead, but her cheeks had regained some of their color and her expression was peaceful.

Something inside him shifted.

He stepped into the room, and she must have sensed him because her eyes fluttered open. A small smile curved her pink lips.

"I didn't mean to wake you." He took a step closer, letting his fingers brush against the cotton blanket on the bed. "How are you?" he asked, his voice low. Something about hospitals made him feel melancholy. Perhaps it had to do with watching his father waste away from liver failure in one.

"I've been better."

Yellow-greenish bruising blossomed under each eye. Anger burned inside him. She could have been killed.

Suddenly aware of the flowers he was holding, he offered them to her. "For you."

Rebecca took the bouquet and brushed it under her nose. A faint smile graced her lips. "They're beautiful."

"Let me find something to put them in." He held up his finger, ran out to the nurses' station and came back with a pitcher. He filled it with water from the bathroom, then plunked the flowers in it, plastic wrap and all.

A smile lit Rebecca's eyes. "Thank you." She lifted her hand and gingerly touched the dressing on her forehead. "The nurse told me Katie and Grace are okay." There was a question in her tone. "Did you take them to my brother's house?"

"Actually," Jake said, sitting down in the pleather chair next to her bed, "Katie and Grace are with Samuel in the waiting room at the end of the hall. The nurse said they could stop in briefly if you felt up to a few visitors."

"I do." She struggled to push herself up with her elbows and winced. She lay back down. "It would make me feel better to see for myself that they're okay."

Jake rested his elbows on the edge of her bed and his fingers lingered inches from the tubes running into the back of her hand. "I'll get them in a minute, but first we need to talk."

She slowly turned her head on the pillow to fully face him and lifted her eyebrows as if to say, "What?"

"You're going to have to make a statement to the sheriff."

Rebecca pressed her lips together but still didn't say anything.

"Someone tried to kill you."

She stared at him, her eyes lacking both shock and fear.

"Samuel is also going to have to talk to the sheriff. The events this morning won't allow me to have you resolve this through your Amish neighbors. Law enforcement must be involved."

Rebecca tried again to sit up by pushing her elbows under her, but she collapsed back on the mattress. "*You* don't have the authority to tell me anything. This is my life. My family."

The sudden harshness of her words sliced through him. Confused by her anger, he dared touch the back of her hand, cautious of the tubes. "I need to make sure you're safe."

"I imagine this would also make a great research paper for you. A nice—what do they call it?—a feather in your cap? Lots of publicity for you. Professor Burke stumbles upon drugs on an Amish widow's farm." She scrunched up her nose. "Imagine when they connect this all to Willard, the Amish murderer."

Rebecca closed her eyes and pulled her hands over her midsection in a protective gesture.

"I'm sorry. The sheriff needs to talk to you."

A single tear leaked from the corner of her eye.

Jake stood, pushing back the chair, its wooden legs dragging across the worn linoleum. He tamped down the conflicting emotions welling inside him.

Did she really think that little of him? That he'd use this information for a research paper?

"If it's okay with you, I'll bring in the kids now."

Without saying a word, Rebecca nodded.

Katie's chatter floated down the hall to Rebecca. She touched her forehead and wished she could somehow hide her injury. She didn't want to worry the girls.

Rebecca fumbled with the remote the nurse had showed her and she moved the head of the bed up a few more inches. Squaring her shoulders, she hoped she appeared stronger than she felt.

The professor appeared in the doorway, then stepped aside to allow her children to enter the room before him. Samuel held his little sisters' hands. *He's such a good big brother.* Rebecca quickly swiped at a tear, frustrated with how close to the surface her emotions lurked. The reason she had lashed out at the professor.

"Hi, *Mem*," Samuel said sheepishly. Rebecca forced a smile, but suddenly the memory of the dark shadow raising his arm to slam something down on her head came to mind.

An oppressive weight squeezed her lungs and she turned to stare out the window. Soft white clouds floated across the pale blue fall sky. She wanted nothing more than to go home and forget about this mess.

Neh, not her Samuel. He wouldn't have hurt her. Not this young man who was protectively ushering his little sisters into her hospital room with whispered words of reassurance. She had heard him when they entered the door: "*Mem*'s okay. She'll be better and home soon."

Grace broke free from her big brother's grasp and ran over to the bed. *"Mem!"* She threw herself down on the bed and buried her face in Rebecca's knees.

Katie, the quieter of the two, wandered over to stand next to her mother and sister.

"I'm okay, girls. I should be home soon. Is everything okay?"

Grace nodded slowly.

Then Rebecca turned to Samuel, who stood at the end of the bed. "Are you okay with the girls?" She trusted him, she truly did.

He nodded, the look in his eyes hard to read under the shadow of his straw hat.

Muffled voices sounded in the hallway outside her door. The sheriff strolled in, a small smile curving the corners of his mouth. He touched a black unit on his shoulder and the voices stopped.

"Didn't know you had a full house." The sheriff took a step back. "I could come back later."

Rebecca gently brushed her hand across Grace's hair and the little girl lifted her head. Rebecca forced a smile that hurt the inside of her head. "Go with your big brother to the waiting room. Sheriff Maxwell wants to talk to me." She looked up and locked gazes with Samuel.

He bowed his head and reached for Katie's hand, then Grace's.

"There are too many people in this room," a nurse said as she strode in. She stopped short upon seeing the sheriff. Then she hiked her chin and glared pointedly at each of the offenders. "I'm sorry, Sheriff Maxwell, but Mrs. Fisher needs to rest. She has a concussion."

"I'll just be a minute."

"A minute." The nurse turned and left the room.

Rebecca's family said their goodbyes, and Samuel ushered the two girls out, their Amish dresses and bonnets out of place against the sterility of the modern hospital room.

The professor touched Rebecca's arm. "I'll be outside if you need me."

"I'd like you to stay."

The sheriff nodded in assent.

"I have a few questions," Sheriff Maxwell said.

Samuel slowed up at the door with his sisters. "Samuel, please take your sisters to the waiting room." Her daughters didn't need to hear this.

"What do you know about the marijuana crops growing on your land?"

Something about the way the sheriff said *your* land unnerved Rebecca. She folded over the corner of the blanket and ran her pinched fingers along its edge. "I hired Uri and Jonas Yoder to help on the farm. Yesterday, Samuel told us he'd discovered they had been using our land to grow these horrible plants."

The sheriff scratched his jaw. "The Yoder brothers tell me your son was the one who planted the marijuana. They claim they knew nothing about the plants since they were tucked in a back corner of your land."

Rebecca smoothed the folded edge of the blanket. The dull pain in her head grew to an unbearable thump. "I... They..." She crossed her arms over her middle. "Last night we went to the Yoders' house and the boys claimed my son was involved, but they were using that as an excuse."

The sheriff wrapped his hand around the metal bar of the footboard. "Rebecca you've had a few rough years."

She felt her mouth grow dry.

"Have you considered that Samuel *might be* responsible?" he continued.

She blinked slowly, sensing the professor's watchful gaze. Did everyone think she lacked good judgment? She had, after all, married a murderer.

Rebecca couldn't squeeze out any words, fearing her emotions would get the best of her.

"Samuel's a good kid," the professor said. Relief swept over her. *Yes, yes he is.*

"I don't think he'd get mixed up with drugs," the professor continued. "From my experience, I've had no indication he's been involved with the drugs in Apple Creek."

"What are your impressions of Uri and Jonas Yoder?" The sheriff tapped his fingers on his thigh.

The professor stuffed his hands into his pockets and shook his head. "I had no indication that they were involved with drugs either. But my time with any of the Amish youth is limited."

The sheriff nodded his head slowly, as if considering

all this. "I'm sending a crew over to the farm to destroy the crops."

Rebecca nodded quickly, immediately regretting the motion as a new wave of pain crashed over her. "That's what I was trying to do when I was attacked."

"You didn't see your attacker?"

"No." She threaded her fingers together, unease tickling her throat.

"Rebecca, I know you've had a tough time of it, but I want you to know that state forfeiture laws state that any property connected to a crime *can* be confiscated."

"Confiscated?" the professor asked, the alarm in his voice setting her nerves on edge.

The sheriff cut a sidelong glance to the professor. "Yes, and if the drugs that led to Elmer's crash can be traced back to illegal activity on your farm, you would also be liable. And there's prison to consider."

If the sheriff had come here to scare her, he could consider his visit a colossal success. She moved to place one hand to her mouth, but the wires on her hand got caught on the side rail. A painful tug reminded her of her injuries, and she dropped her hand. The professor gently untangled the wires and placed her hand by her side. He grazed the skin on the back of her hand softly with the pad of his thumb before releasing her hand.

Rebecca glanced up at the professor through a watery haze. She couldn't talk for fear of having a total meltdown.

"Can this wait until she's feeling better?" the professor asked. "This is all news to Rebecca. She had no knowledge of the crops prior to yesterday."

The sheriff stepped toward the door. "I don't want you to blindly protect Samuel. There's a lot at stake here for you *and* your little girls."

A dull thud pulsed behind her eyes. "I am not *blindly*

protecting anyone." Did the sheriff think Samuel had planted the marijuana and tried to stop her this morning? Her mind flashed to the shadow bearing down on her. Samuel couldn't have possibly—

"I did it," Samuel blurted from the doorway, where he must have been secretly listening to their conversation. "My *mem* had nothing to do with this. She didn't even know about the crops until I told the professor last night. I'm the *only* one responsible."

With a trembling hand, Rebecca peeled back the white covers of her hospital bed. She swung her feet around and shook her head, refusing the professor's assistance.

Standing on shaky legs, Rebecca held out her arm to Samuel. "You need to forgive yourself."

Her son bowed his head and tapped the frame of the door with the tip of his boot. The image of the little boy she had first come to know haunted her memory. She loved him as her own. Her heart ached for him.

She moved slowly across the cold hospital floor that seemed to tilt with each step. She was aware of the professor hovering next to her.

"You need to forgive yourself for whatever you feel you did wrong when it came to your father," she repeated. "Your *dat* was a bad man. Not you."

Samuel hung his head, unwilling to look her in the eyes.

"You saved lives by helping law enforcement get him off the street." She reached up to touch Samuel, but her arm dropped to her side. "Forgive yourself. Move on. Don't try to ease your guilt by taking blame for the marijuana crops in some misguided attempt to protect me. It's not going to solve anything."

Samuel sniffed and his shoulders shook.

"I know you would never hurt me." She touched the bandage on her head. "I know it wasn't your idea to plant

the marijuana on the farm." She shook her head and immediately regretted it. "I know that's not you. *Elmer* made
his own bad choices. *Not* you. Forgive yourself."

Little footsteps sounded and Katie and Grace ran into
the room, then hung back, as if sensing something intense
was going on.

"Son," the sheriff finally spoke up, "are you confessing
to growing the marijuana?"

Her son's eyes moved to his little sisters, then to his
mem. Samuel nodded. "Yes, I'm responsible. My *mem* had
nothing to do with it."

"*Neh*, Samuel. Stop this foolishness," Rebecca pleaded.

"I'm guilty." Samuel stepped forward.

The sheriff grabbed Samuel's arm. "I'm going to have
to take you down to the station." The sheriff started rattling off something about a right to an attorney, but all
Rebecca could focus on was the metal handcuffs binding
Samuel's wrists.

The world suddenly grew very dark. Rebecca sensed
the professor's hand on her elbow as she backed up until
the back of her legs connected with the bed. She planted
a hand on the mattress to steady herself. "Don't do this."

The sheriff glanced her way, a look of contrition in
his eyes. "I'll call Jake to let you know what's going on.
Okay?"

When she didn't answer—couldn't answer—the sheriff
added, "I'll make sure he's okay in lockup."

Rebecca heard soothing words from the professor but
couldn't make heads or tails of them. Didn't the sheriff
know that nothing would ever be okay again?

NINE

Jake swiped the back of his hand across his forehead and squinted up at the sun hanging low in the sky. A few days had passed since Samuel's arrest and subsequent release on bail. The Fisher family had a lot on their minds. Fortunately, Rebecca had been released from the hospital. She dismissed the doctor's orders to rest, insisting that farm life went on.

With aching muscles, Jake maneuvered the wagon into place behind the barn with Samuel's help. Then Samuel rode the tractor—without rubber on its tires—into the far corner of the barn. The two men had worked in relative silence most of the day, both in tune with the work at hand. Jake had done some gardening as a kid, but he had no idea he'd enjoy working the land so much.

When Samuel emerged from the barn, he made a straight line for the house. Jake called out to him. "We need to talk."

Samuel kept walking.

"You can't ignore the situation. The Amish might like to keep the law separate, but you're caught in the legal system now. It will *not* go away."

Samuel spun around and adjusted his straw hat low on his forehead to hide his eyes. "Who says I'm ignoring it? I promised you wouldn't lose your bail money. I'll be there on the court date." He rubbed a hand across the back of his neck. "Any idea when that will be?"

"It hasn't been set yet. The lawyer I hired will let us know."

Samuel slowly shook his head. "Why are you doing all this for us? It's not your problem."

"I don't think you're guilty. I think you're trying to protect your mother by taking the blame. Confessing to something you didn't do is not going to help you or your mother. The right people need to be punished."

Samuel clenched his jaw.

"Someone's been threatening you and your mom."

"You think you're so smart?" Samuel's words came out clipped with frustration and anger. "If you're so smart, you'd stay away from here, too. How do you think having an *Englisher* work the farm appears to our Amish neighbors?"

"Your *mother* needed help. I'm helping you guys harvest the crops now that you've lost the farmhands."

The young man pressed his lips together and shook his head. He had obviously said his piece.

Jake rolled his aching shoulders and decided to change the subject. "I haven't had this much physical exertion since my army days."

Samuel's expression softened. "You were in the army?"

"Yes, I wanted to serve my country and it helped pay for college."

"Maybe I could follow that path and go to college. Tommy seems to think I couldn't get a decent job without a college degree."

Jake studied the young man's thoughtful expression. A criminal record would also prove limiting, but he decided not to go there. "Do you agree with the Amish stance on being a conscientious objector?"

Samuel straightened his back and tried to take on an air of nonchalance, but Jake saw through his false bravado.

"I'm not baptized yet. I don't have to follow the Amish rules."

"True, but going into the army would be difficult for someone like you."

"You think I'm weak."

"I didn't say that. It's not a decision to make lightly."

"If I go to jail, the decision will be made for me, right?" Samuel's biting tone was at odds with the fear that flitted in the depths of his eyes. He shrugged and said, "I'm going to clean up before dinner." He spun on his heels and marched toward the house.

Jake stood and watched the young man until Rebecca caught his eye. She was walking across the field toward him, wisps of hair loose around the front of her head, like a halo glowing in the soft light from the setting sun. They had all put in a long day in the fields, riding the tractor with rudimentary equipment, harvesting the corn for feed. Rebecca had insisted on helping despite Jake's protests that she rest. The Amish were apparently made of hearty stock.

When she reached him, she smiled shyly. "You're a natural." She fingered the strings of her bonnet, then dropped her hand.

"Maybe it's in my blood." Both his parents were Amish, after all.

"I can't thank you enough. Will you stay for dinner?"

He scrunched up his face, realizing how hungry he was. He had been too busy to think about it earlier. "I would hate to intrude."

Rebecca waved her hand in dismissal.

"When did you have time to make dinner?"

"I made a shepherd's pie from some leftovers in the icebox. I hope that's okay."

"Sounds great."

He followed Rebecca up the worn path to the house. She slowed before they reached the porch. "You were talking to Samuel. How does he seem? He hardly speaks to me."

Jake wanted to take her hands in his, to reassure her, but he resisted. "He's sticking to the same story. I hope he changes it before the court date."

Rebecca lowered her eyes and nodded. "I can't thank you enough for intervening on his behalf. If not for you, I fear he would have been overwhelmed by the *English* legal system." She let out a mirthless laugh. "For an Amish woman, I've had my fair share of legal troubles."

This time Jake did reach out and touch her wrist briefly. "I'll help you however I can."

"Denki." The Pennsylvania Dutch word for *thank you* rolled off her pink lips.

"You're very welcome."

When they entered the kitchen, Grace and Katie had finished setting the table. Grace smiled up at him. "Oh, we'll set another plate." She stretched up and grabbed a white plate from the cabinet.

Rebecca held out her hand. "You can wash up. The bathroom is at the back of the house."

After Jake washed his hands, he joined them at the long pine table. He had been invited to join an Amish family a time or two as part of his studies, but he had always felt as if the family was putting on a show for his benefit. Only when he joined Rebecca and her family did he feel comfortable.

He looked over at Rebecca and she caught him watching her. Well, almost comfortable.

Samuel sat across the table from him. An aura of teenage angst rolled off him. Jake supposed he had gotten all he was going to get from the young man today.

Samuel put his hands in his lap and they all followed suit. They bowed their heads in silent prayer. Samuel was the first to raise his head and pick up his fork, signaling it was time to eat.

"How was school today, girls?" Rebecca asked.

Grace smiled. "We got to play outside at recess. The teacher thinks we might not have many nice days left before it snows."

Her mother laughed. "Did you learn anything?"

"Our teacher Miss Marian is getting married."

Rebecca caught the professor smiling.

"I suppose some things are universal. Kids love recess and their teachers," Jake said.

Rebecca took a scoop of potatoes with her fork and stopped midway to her mouth. "Girls, did you know Professor Burke is a teacher?"

They both looked at him without saying anything.

"*He* doesn't teach little kids. He teaches big people in college."

"Amy's older brother left home and went to college. He's now under the *Bann*," Katie said, her tone ominous, as if at her tender age she already understood the full repercussions of being shunned.

Jake fidgeted with the knife, pushing it under the edge of his plate. Shunning was losing popularity in a number of Amish communities, but some Amish parents still felt it was the only way to encourage baptized members to return to the fold. Some parents used it to encourage their child to be baptized.

Tough love.

Katie swallowed a mouthful of food and asked, "Is being a professor bad?"

Rebecca laughed nervously. "No, it's just something Amish people wouldn't do. We only are allowed an eighth grade education."

"Why?" Grace asked.

"Because that's all we really need. You'll learn everything necessary to be a good wife and *mem* at the Amish schoolhouse."

"*They* want to make sure they can keep us close," Samuel bit out. "*They* want us to have no choice but to stay." He tossed down his fork and pushed back his chair. The legs scraped against the wooden floor, making a sharp squeal.

Rebecca slowly closed her eyes, as if gathering strength. Samuel stomped up the stairs. The young girls stared after their brother with shocked expressions.

"Girls," Rebecca said, "your brother has been rude and I will deal with him later." She paused, perhaps to quell the shakiness in her voice. "Anyway, the Amish school will teach you everything you need to know." Rebecca watched her daughters with a look of hope and sadness in her eyes. Jake knew how important it was that her daughters stayed in the Amish community, especially with her eldest pushing all the boundaries.

"What if I decide I want to be really smart like the professor? Will you stop talking to me?" Katie said with a hint of what the future teenage Katie might be like.

Rebecca's jaw tightened and she blinked slowly. "My wish for you is that you grow up to love being in Apple Creek as much as I do."

"When Miss Hannah married Sheriff Maxwell, she moved to a house in Apple Creek, but she's not Amish anymore. If you marry Professor Burke, can we get a house near them? We could play with Emma and Sarah every day after school."

Rebecca picked up her fork and stabbed at her mashed potatoes. "Girls, eat before your food gets cold."

Rebecca washed the last plate and handed it to the professor to dry. He placed it in the cabinet and hung the damp dishtowel on the hook.

Rebecca turned around and leaned back, curving her hands around the edge of the counter. "My husband never helped with chores inside the house." She lifted a shoulder to shrug. "I suppose most Amish men know their place is on the farm." She lowered her gaze, suddenly feeling flushed. "Or more and more nowadays at the factory or building swing sets down the road. Things are changing fast." She didn't say more because Willard's nasty words rang in her head. That had been his battle cry. Things were changing too much. We had to hold on to the old ways.

The Amish must remain separate.

Her stomach ached. She hated that she agreed with her husband's general premise, yet she'd never resort to Willard's extremes.

The professor smiled and Rebecca worked her lower lip. Her growing feelings of affection were getting difficult to ignore.

"I suppose I should go." He apparently sensed her unease.

"Maybe—" she couldn't believe she was about to say this "—we could sit and talk on the porch for a bit?" Oh, what was she doing? What kind of example was she setting for her daughters? She should escort the professor out the door to go home for the night.

The professor held out his hand. "After you."

She was lonely and longed for adult companionship. The nights were too long with all her racing thoughts about Samuel's future.

Her future.

As Rebecca and the professor passed through the house, she called up the stairs. "Girls, I'll be on the front porch. Get changed and you can read a bit before bed."

Footsteps scampered overhead and she heard the bathroom door slam shut. No doubt Katie had beaten Grace to the bathroom. She smiled at the ordinariness of everyday life. What she wouldn't do to have all of life be that simple.

Rebecca stepped onto the porch and sat in the rocker. A warm fall breeze swept across her skin and with it the scent of dried hay and freshly harvested crops.

The professor lowered himself into the chair next to hers and sighed contentedly. "I could get used to this."

Rebecca laughed. "The path not chosen."

"At the time, it wasn't for me to choose. My parents left their Amish community and eloped."

"Were they happy?"

The professor settled back in his chair and made an indistinguishable sound in the back of his throat. "I imagine they were happy in the beginning. They were young and free of all the rules of the *Ordnung* for the first time in their lives. They were together."

Rebecca stared over the farm. The bright moon cast the land in a warm glow. A deep but good tired settled around her. Momentary peace, compliments of the man sitting next to her. A man who was completely wrong for her.

She shook away the thought. She could never get together with an *Englisher*. It would go against everything she believed in. Every reason she had worked so hard to bring Samuel back into the fold.

She'd be a hypocrite.

A wistfulness in the professor's tone made her pause. Made her realize something. "Did something happen to make your parents regret their decision to leave the Amish community?"

"I never said…" He shook his head and laughed. "I guess I didn't have to say as much." He sighed heavily. "My father was frustrated because he could never get a decent job. He was stuck working minimum-wage jobs because he—"

"Only had an eighth grade education," Rebecca finished for him, realization dawning. "We talked about that over dinner."

"Exactly."

"Is that why you got all that education and teach at a university?" She swatted away a moth fluttering close to her face.

"Yes, I always equated an education with a happy life. My father would sit down every night with a beer in one hand and a remote in the other in front of the TV and mutter something about 'get an education son, because them people hold all the power.'"

The ever-present emptiness inside Rebecca expanded. She was not the only one with a painful past.

"He pretty much gave up on life. Drank himself stupid right until the end."

She was grateful for the cloak of darkness to hide the tears brimming in her eyes.

"He died of liver failure."

"I'm sorry." Nervously, Rebecca played with the folds in her long gown and tucked her bare feet under the rocker. She hated to ask, but curiosity got the best of her. "What about your mom?"

"My mom died when I was ten. From cancer."

Rebecca gasped. "I didn't mean to pry. How horrible. I'm so, so sorry."

"My parents couldn't afford anything but the basic treatment. I suppose they could have gotten more care if they weren't naive to the system. It was all foreign to them." He scrubbed a hand over his face and his features grew pinched. "My dad's drinking got worse the sicker my mom got…"

He let out a quick breath. "I've never told anyone the story of my life. I guess I never wanted to share my past with anyone before."

"I'm glad you told me. I feel closer to you." She glanced away, suddenly feeling very self-conscious.

He reached out and covered her hand on the arm of the chair and gave it a gentle squeeze. "Life gets complicated sometimes."

Keenly aware of his hand on hers, she glanced over her shoulder at the door. "I know. I hope we can get Samuel out of trouble. I really appreciate your putting up his bail." She slid her hand out from under his and wrapped her arms around her midsection. "The thought of him in jail…"

He leaned toward her. "I'll help you in every way I can." He tilted his head. "But when I said life gets complicated, I wasn't talking about Samuel."

Rebecca glanced up into his warm brown eyes. Her pulse beat steadily in her ears and her skin flushed warm.

Get up. Move away from him.

She couldn't. This gentle man held her heart. She sucked in a breath, waiting for him to continue.

He leaned closer, his breath whispering across her cheek. A smile tilted the corners of his mouth. He hesitated a minute, as if waiting for her reaction. Her permission. A boldness she'd never known surged through her. She reached up and touched his cheek; the scruff of his unshaven jaw felt rough under her palm.

He leaned in closer and brushed a gentle kiss across

her lips. Then he pulled back and angled his head, studying her.

Closing her eyes briefly, she dropped her hand into her lap and wrung her hands. She opened her eyes and met his.

"Should I apologize for kissing you?"

No, no, no.

"We're from two different worlds." Her voice came out in a strained whisper. This entire situation was foreign to her.

A twinkle lit his eyes. "So, that's a no?" He laughed.

Rebecca smiled. She could get used to this man's easygoing ways. His warm heart. His companionship.

Too bad a relationship between them would never happen.

Jake scooted forward in his rocker and curled his hands in an effort to keep them to himself. He was having trouble containing a smile. Rebecca had her hands wrapped around the arms of the chair and looked as if she was ready to bolt. He really should apologize, but if he was truly honest with himself, he wasn't sorry.

The memory of her soft lips on his. Her clean scent. Her soft skin.

Definitely not sorry.

But he hated to see her filled with angst. And he didn't want to risk having her send him away forever.

"Did I overstep my place?" he asked in a husky voice.

Rebecca lifted her fingers and touched her lips. An emotion he couldn't quite define flittered in the depths of her eyes.

"It's my fault."

"Your fault?" Intrigued, Jake leaned back in his rocker and relaxed his hands. "Because you're beautiful?"

She lifted her hand in dismissal. "Please. You're embarrassing me." She turned her face away from him and smoothed a hand along the edge of her bonnet. Slowly she turned to face him, clutching her hands in her lap. "This kiss can't *mean* anything. We have no future together."

She was right. The pain in her eyes cut to his core. "I didn't mean to cause you any more stress."

The thought of encouraging Rebecca to leave the Amish didn't bring him joy any more than saying goodbye to her would. His father had convinced his mother to leave and he had experienced firsthand the sadness that had ensued.

"I hope I didn't destroy our friendship," Jake said, a muscle working in his jaw.

Rebecca bowed her head. "Don't blame yourself. I feel the connection between us, too."

Jake's heartbeat spiked at her admission. Yet, still, he could never ask her to leave the Amish.

Rebecca met his gaze, a look of clarity in her eyes. "I should have never put you in this position, Professor Burke. I came to you because I was worried about Samuel." A tendril of hair that had escaped her bonnet fluttered in the breeze. "I don't want you to feel responsible for me every time something goes wrong. It's not your responsibility."

"I don't mind."

Rebecca shook her head slowly. "You're a good man. But I need to rely on my own community. Not an outsider."

"An outsider, huh?" Jake laughed before giving her a wounded look and covering his midsection as if he had been punched in the gut.

Rebecca's brow furrowed. "Are you not feeling well?"

Jake lifted an eyebrow. "We really are from two different worlds."

"Yes, we are. I don't think it's a good idea for you to keep coming around."

A rustling sounded from the yard and Jake rose to his

feet and squinted into the darkness. Lester Lapp, the bishop's son, stepped into the soft light flowing from her house.

Rebecca was slower to her feet. She walked to the railing and wrapped her hands around it. "Hello, Lester. It's late to be calling."

"I have business to discuss."

"Business with me? You haven't come by my farm since before Willard's arrest."

Lester adjusted his hat on his head, as if trying to gather his thoughts. "He killed my brother."

The soft gasp from Rebecca made Jake's hands twitch. He longed to pull her into an embrace. Comfort her.

Lester held up his hand. "I'm sorry. I should have been more sensitive. I have forgiven him, but I still struggle with my loss."

She bowed her head and whispered, "I understand."

Lester gave Jake a pointed look, but turned back to Rebecca. "The bishop hasn't been feeling well. I'm here on his behalf."

"I hope your father is feeling better soon."

Lester nodded. *"Denki."* He took a few steps closer, put his foot on the bottom porch step and rested his elbow on the railing. "The bishop would like Samuel to meet with him and a few of the church elders."

All the color drained out of her face and Jake immediately felt defensive. "I don't believe he's guilty of the things—"

"He's confessed to?" Lester interrupted with a smug quirk of his lips.

Rebecca wrung her hands in front of her. "Samuel's afraid of something. He's trying to protect me." Her words came out rushed and flustered. "And he's not baptized yet. The church elders have been known to overlook transgressions of our *youngie.*"

Lester removed his hat and gave her a look Jake could only read as "you've got to be kidding me."

"Growing marijuana on God's land is more than a *little* transgression."

"Rebecca's been through a lot," Jake spoke up. "Now is not a good time."

The Amish man wiped his forehead, then settled his hat back on his head. "Perhaps Mrs. Fisher should remember she *is* a baptized member of this community."

A muscle started ticking in Jake's jaw, but despite the fury racing through his brain, he got hold of his emotions. Blasting this man with a piece of his mind wasn't going to help Rebecca.

"I was telling the professor he needs to find new subjects to study." Rebecca's voice was surprisingly firm.

Lester held up his hand. "Is that all this is?"

Jake slowly descended the steps. "Good night, Rebecca."

"Good night, Professor." She paused a brief moment. "Good night, Lester." Rebecca turned around and went inside, obviously unwilling to discuss this further with either of them.

In the front yard, Lester turned to Jake. "I trust you're not courting Rebecca."

"Courting?" Jake asked noncommittally before changing the subject. "You are the bishop's son." Jake knew who Lester was, but he was buying time to formulate his thoughts…his words.

Lester tipped his hat.

"How often does someone join the Amish community?" From his own research, Jake knew it wasn't often.

Lester's eyes flared wide under the moonlight. "Join the Amish?" He let out a bark of laughter that grated on Jake's nerves. "Are *you* considering joining us?"

Jake didn't trust himself to answer, suspecting that clocking the arrogant man wouldn't win him any favors.

"You don't join the Amish like you're joining a country club. This is our community. A way of life. A serious commitment."

"I am very familiar with the Amish. I have been studying the Amish and teaching at the university for years."

"So," Lester said, the single word dripping with sarcasm, "is this the last step in your research? To join the Amish?" He shook his head and scoffed. "Through your vast research you should have already figured all this out."

Jake blinked slowly, trying to tamp down his emotions. "I know outsiders joining the Amish is unusual, but it has been done."

Lester's eyes locked on the front door of Rebecca's home. "The church elders will look unkindly on a man choosing to join the Amish for the wrong reasons."

Jake kept his thoughts to himself.

"Joining because you want to court the widow Fisher is not valid grounds." Lester took a few steps away, then turned around. "Rebecca was right. You shouldn't keep coming around here."

Jake narrowed his gaze, more than a little annoyed that Lester had obviously been eavesdropping on them before he'd made his presence known.

TEN

While Jake was driving home, he realized he'd never be able to sleep so he decided to go to his campus office and catch up on some work. He'd had his graduate teaching assistant cover his class today, but he couldn't keep doing that. Not if he still wanted a job.

Jake easily found parking in the nearly empty lot. It was after nine, a few students were crisscrossing the campus on the quiet fall evening.

"Hi, Professor Burke," a young woman said as he strolled across the quad to his office in the Stevenson building. He waved at her as he remembered his first day on campus a few years ago. He thought he had finally made it. He thought he should finally be happy because he had the education, he had the job, all the things that his father lacked.

So why had happiness—real happiness—eluded him until now? Until Rebecca had come into his life? The quiet Amish woman had made him feel content. But was Lester right? Were his motives to join the Amish pure or just a way to remain close to Rebecca?

Jake pulled open the large door to his building. Guilt pinged him. He'd had no right to kiss Rebecca. To take advantage of her. She was vulnerable.

Jake tried but couldn't forget the feel of her soft lips, her quick intake of breath, the fresh smell of windswept hair...

Wrapped in the memory of the kiss, he walked down the long hallway, his footsteps sounding on the marble floor. As he approached room 214, he noticed a light filtering out from under the door. His head jerked back.

Jake turned the handle on the door; it was unlocked. The computer at Tommy's desk was on, but he saw no sign of his assistant. He strolled into the office and heard a voice.

"Yeah, I'll figure something out."

Jake turned the corner and saw Tommy sitting on the floor of his office, leaning against the wall with his legs stretched out in front of him. Tommy looked up when Jake entered the room. "Gotta go," he said into the phone. He ended the call and scrambled to his feet.

"Hey, Professor, what are you doing here?" Tommy moved around to the desk. The chair squeaked when he plopped down into it and leaned back.

"I suppose I could ask you the same thing."

"I come in here to use the computer when the computer lab's too busy." Tommy wiggled the mouse and the screen came to life. Some Word document was on the screen. "My laptop bit the dust and I can't afford a new one."

Jake waved his hand, indicating it wasn't a problem. He stepped into his office and sat behind his big desk. He moved some of the papers and books around. Once this— all of this—had meant everything to him.

Studying the Amish had made him feel connected, but not in the way that Rebecca made him feel...connected. When he was with Rebecca, he felt as if he was home.

"Professor Burke?"

Jake snapped his attention to the door. Tommy had a look that made Jake think he had called his name a few times.

"What's up, Tommy?"

His assistant jabbed his thumb toward his desk. "I'm going to wrap things up here and call it a night." Tommy leaned across the desk and clicked a few buttons on the computer. "…And sent. Got to love technology. Paper was due by midnight. I submitted it through email."

Jake nodded. He still gave his students the option of handing in a paper or sending him an email.

A slow smile spread across the young man's face. "Everything okay? You look like someone stole your favorite toy."

Jake laughed. "No, just trying to catch up with work here."

"You're spending a lot of time with the Fisher family." It was more a statement than a question. Tommy crossed his arms and leaned his hip on the frame of the doorway. "You're really deep in research mode."

"Mmm" was Jake's only response.

"This whole growing marijuana on the Amish farm will make a great paper. You'll put the Amish Apple Creek community on the map. Kinda like that gunman did with the Amish in Nickel Mines."

Anger started burning deep in Jake's gut, but he didn't want to lash out at Tommy. He was a kid, not exactly socially savvy.

"I'm not going to write about it."

A smirk slashed across Tommy's thin lips. "Really? I thought it would make an interesting paper."

"I want to be respectful." Jake stood, walked around the front of his desk and perched on its corner. "I've been giving her a hand since the Yoder brothers quit. She needed help with the harvest."

"I'm sure some of their Amish neighbors would step up

to the plate." Tommy stuffed something into his backpack and zipped it up. "You're an expert on the Amish. They help one another. You know that."

"The Fishers have felt isolated since Willard Fisher was convicted of murder. Hopefully with time, things will change." *If* Jake stayed away that might help bridge the gap. Rebecca had to learn to rely on her Amish neighbors again. Her Amish neighbors needed time to forgive, even if they never forgot.

Tommy shook his head. "Talk about bad karma with that family. It's like they're a bad-luck magnet. But you know as well as I do that the Amish will eventually find forgiveness in their hearts. Someone will step forward and help them in their time of need."

"One can hope."

Tommy slung his backpack over one shoulder and gave Jake a knowing look. "Forgive me for speaking out of turn, but do you have something for Mrs. Fisher?" He lifted an eyebrow.

Jake couldn't help but laugh. He threaded a hand through his hair. "I enjoy spending time with Rebecca." Jake waved his hand. "But that's it. I'm just helping a person who's having a rough time."

Tommy levered off the doorframe and nodded slowly. "Guard your heart, Professor. Mrs. Fisher...she's gonna break yours." He turned to leave, then muttered over his shoulder. "They always do."

"We are *not* having this conversation."

Tommy turned around to face him. "I can't see you becoming Amish."

"That's what I call jumping to a conclusion without supporting evidence." Jake kept his voice even.

"You'd never give all this up. You've worked too hard."

The young man scrunched up his nose. "You may have a romanticized notion of the Amish from your research, but studying and living it are two different beasts." Tommy adjusted the strap on his shoulder. "Trust me. Been there, done that. Got the T-shirt—or should I say, broad-brimmed hat—to prove it."

The next morning at the diner, Rebecca's head pounded. Not getting enough rest despite her recent injury was bound to do that. Rest was long in coming. After her job at the diner, she still had chores to do on the farm. Samuel had promised to see that his little sisters got to school, and her sister-in-law Gloria would pick them up after school and bring them home after Rebecca's shift.

Rebecca rolled her shoulders, trying to ease out the kinks. She grabbed the milk from the counter, screwed on the lid, then yanked on the lever of the walk-in freezer.

"Hey, hey, hey…" Flo walked up behind her and put a hand on her back. "Dear, unless we plan to plop frozen milk into glasses, we better put that back in the refrigerator."

Rebecca blinked a few times, wondering how she'd ended up standing in front of the freezer with a jug of milk in her hand.

Flo took the milk and put it in the refrigerator. "What's on your mind today? Worried about Samuel?"

Rebecca was *always* worried about Samuel, but something else was pressing on her heart this morning. She looked up, met Flo's warm gaze and smiled.

Flo tilted her head, a pleading look in her eyes. "Dear, if you're gonna spill it, you better do it soon before the breakfast crowd gets here. Then you're going to have to hold your peace until midmorning." She twirled her hand in a get-on-with-it gesture. "And you are *not* going to leave here today without telling me what's on your mind."

Rebecca smoothed a hand across the edge of her bonnet and her mouth went dry. "The professor and I visited for a bit on the porch last night."

Her friend's eyebrows shot up. "You did, did you?"

Rebecca couldn't help but smile at her friend's response. Oh, how she wished it was as simple as Flo thought it was.

Flo crossed her arms and leaned her hip on the silver counter, settling in for all the gossip. "Did something happen?" Flo had a way of pinning her with a penetrating gaze. Flo's hand flew to her mouth. "Oh, something happened. Did he kiss you?"

Rebecca had no plans to kiss and tell.

"I didn't mean to embarrass you, dear. You're young and pretty and you have your life in front of you." She leaned in close. "I say go for it."

Rebecca laughed. "Go for what? You know how conservative the Amish are. He'd have to become Amish for us to have a future."

Flo ran a finger across her bottom lip. "There is that." Her shoulders sagged. "Poor girl, you have that handsome man paying you visits, yet you're bound to the Amish ways." She bit her lower lip and furrowed her brow. "Are you sure? Maybe a fresh start would be a good thing for you."

Rebecca knew there was no way her friend would understand. "A fresh start would mean leaving everything I've ever known."

The bell on the door jangled, indicating their first breakfast customers, a handful of retired men who stopped in five days out of the week to chat.

"I'll get this table." Flo walked toward the dining room,

then glanced over her shoulder. "Considering everything you've been through, would a fresh start be so bad?"

After another long day at the diner and a ride home from Flo, Rebecca hung her coat on the hook and turned to see a horse and buggy come up the driveway. She hustled to the front door and greeted her daughters. Gloria walked them to the door briskly through the steady rain while Mark waved from the buggy.

"Thank you," Rebecca yelled to her brother, then smiled at Gloria. "I can't thank you enough. I appreciate you bringing them home."

Gloria touched each of the girls' bonnets with a tender look on her face.

The two girls ran into the house, shaking off their damp coats.

"Go on up and get into your nightclothes," Rebecca said to her daughters. She missed seeing their sweet faces all day long.

Once the girls had pounded up the stairs, Gloria leaned in close and whispered, "It wonders me if we should let the girls stay at our house during the week. Since you have to work. We'd love to have them."

Rebecca frowned and she cast her glance toward the floor. "I'm their *mem*. They need to stay here."

"*Yah*, well, I know you're their *mem*," Gloria said, compassion in her tone. "It's too much back and forth. The girls might feel more settled. It will be right like they're home."

Rebecca wrung her hands. "Why do you think the girls aren't settled?"

"I can tell I've offended you. I know you're doing the best you can. The girls need stability. With everything going on with Samuel, maybe it's best if they weren't around that."

"Samuel is their brother. Samuel is innocent." Rebecca hesitated a minute. He was innocent, wasn't he? What if he went to jail all the same? Her poor family would be the subject of more finger-pointing.

Rebecca let out a long, slow breath and ran a hand over her face. Her eyes felt gritty from a long day at work. Another day in which she had been away from her family.

Her little girls.

"Maybe they could stay with us until things settle down. I'd hate for something to happen to them," Gloria said.

Suddenly that piece of apple pie with ice cream Rebecca had had before she'd left the diner didn't seem like such a good idea.

"What do you mean, 'something happen to them'?"

Gloria bowed her head and her cheeks turned pink. "Many evil things have surrounded your family."

Rebecca gasped. She struggled to find the words. "You don't think they're safe here?" Apprehension knotted her stomach.

Through the open front door, Rebecca could see her brother sitting in the buggy, his broad-brimmed hat pulled down low on his forehead as he stared straight ahead, squinting against the wind and rain blowing in the open sides. Served him right for taking the coward's way out and leaving his wife to broach this difficult subject.

"Grace asked me if they could still visit if you married the professor."

"What?"

"She's worried that she'll be leaving the Amish community. She's worried she won't get to see her cousins, but she seemed somewhat comforted by the idea she could still play with your friend Hannah's children."

Rebecca blinked slowly, trying to absorb it all. She laughed, a nervous sound. "Kids get silly ideas. The professor has been helping me. There's nothing romantic going on." The little white lie burned on her lips.

"Perhaps things would be less complicated for you if you spent more time with the Amish than with the English."

Little feet sounded on the stairs and Rebecca spun around. Grace descended the stairs with a doll under her arm. "Can I play with my doll before bed?"

Rebecca smiled at her sweet daughter. "Of course. Let me finish talking to *Aenti* Gloria. I'll be right up to hear all about your day."

Rebecca watched her daughter climb the stairs, then when she was satisfied the little girl was out of hearing distance, she turned to Gloria. "I was desperate when I approached the professor."

"Why didn't you come to us?" The hint of accusation in her sister-in-law's question heated Rebecca's skin.

"When was the last time you spent time with Samuel?"

Gloria bristled, but didn't say anything.

"The professor has been meeting with the Amish youth. I thought he could provide insight into Samuel's behavior."

"I've never liked the idea of outsiders coming into our community and studying us."

Rebecca laughed. "Me neither, but the professor is a good man."

Gloria raised a curious eyebrow.

"His parents were Amish."

"Really?"

"They left before they got married."

Gloria lowered her voice. "You're not planning on leaving, are you?" There was an ominous quality to her voice.

Rebecca slowly shook her head. "I'm not leaving. You know that. I've been working hard to guide Samuel on the right path. Why would you ever think I was planning on being a fence jumper?" An iciness sped through her. "Did the church elders come to you? Did they put you up to this?"

Her dear sister-in-law nodded. "Everyone's worried."

"I wish the elders had jumped in to condemn the members who have been harassing us. We've felt all alone."

"I believe those incidents were addressed. The community was devastated by your husband's actions."

Tears bit at the back of Rebecca's eyes. "They were addressed, but not with the tenacity that they have been addressing the issues with Samuel. Lester stopped by and told us the bishop wants to meet with Samuel. I'm reluctant to send him over there for fear Samuel will run away for good."

"You can't ignore the request."

"I don't plan to, but I do plan to go with him. The last thing I want him to feel is ganged up on."

Gloria gave her a sad smile. "You are a much stronger woman than I am. Please be careful not to turn your back on the Amish way, too."

Rebecca furrowed her brow. "Why would you say that? I have no intention of running away. I only plan to protect my son."

"You are a kind and forgiving woman. Just be sure Samuel is worthy of your kindness."

Rebecca clamped her mouth shut, unwilling to lash out on a woman who had shown her and her daughters much kindness. She took a step toward the door. "I've had a long day and I'm tired. Thank you for bringing the girls home."

Gloria stared at her a moment, before smiling tightly and nodding. *"Guten Nacht."*

Rebecca saw her sister-in-law out the door and then dropped down in one of the rockers, her knees weak with the turn of events. Her heart might be confused over her feelings for the professor, but she was steadfast in her determination to live the Amish way. And to set her son on the right path.

She tugged at the straps on her bonnet. She had two daughters to consider. If she had any hope of keeping them on the straight and narrow, she'd have to be stronger. She'd have to ignore the feelings she had for a man who was absolutely wrong for her and she'd have to stand strong against Samuel's misbehavior.

Rebecca prayed she could save her son. But she could no longer be weak. Not if she didn't want to risk her two young daughters watching with impressionable minds and thinking that flaunting the Amish rules would get nothing but more attention and coddling.

No more.

ELEVEN

A few days later, Rebecca stood by the back door—her stomach twisted in knots—and waited for Samuel to return from his morning chores. She had sent Katie and Grace out to check on the pumpkins in their small garden. Rebecca couldn't bear to see the look of disappointment in their eyes, too.

When Samuel appeared outside the barn, his head slightly bowed, a bead of sweat popped out on her forehead.

Could she really do this?

Her gaze fell to the suitcase inside the door. Samuel's suitcase. The one she had packed for him while he was outside. Rebecca had met with the bishop without Samuel and through the professor, she had gotten approval from the courts for this next course of action. It was her hope to get Samuel away from the negative influence of his local friends while he awaited a court date.

Rebecca glanced at the wall clock. The ride to the bus depot that she had arranged for Samuel would be here soon. The last thing she wanted was for Flo's son to arrive before she had a chance to tell Samuel what was happening.

When Samuel reached the back porch, he slowed and

glanced up at her with a quizzical look on his face. "What's going on?"

"You're going on a trip," Rebecca said, barely able to get the words out of her parched mouth. She pushed open the screen door for her son and he stepped inside.

Samuel's gaze dropped to the worn suitcase on the floor. He took off his hat and tossed it on the hook. A strand of hay in his hair almost broke her heart. She had a flash of meeting Samuel for the first time. He had been a little boy who had lost his mother and had been reluctant to welcome Rebecca into his life. To welcome a second mother.

She immediately second-guessed her bold plan. She was blindsiding him. Maybe she should have warned him.

Samuel brushed past her and into the kitchen to wash his hands. Rebecca followed him.

"I've packed your things for a trip to—"

"You're kicking me out?" His brow furrowed and anger flashed in his eyes. It wrecked her to hurt him like this. She grabbed the back of the chair to steady herself, fearing her weak knees would go out from under her.

She struggled to form the words. She wanted him gone before Grace and Katie came back inside. She didn't want them to witness her sending their big brother away. She wanted time to explain things to her daughters without adding an emotional goodbye scene.

"I've made arrangements for you to stay in an Amish community in the Rochester area. Their church is in communion with ours."

Samuel's brows drew together. "You're kicking me out of my home? *My* home." His jaw trembled. "You said I was your son, but now I know the truth. You've always considered me *Willard's* son. The son of a convicted murderer. I'm no better than my father and you want me out of the house because I'm such a wicked influence."

"That's not true." Her voice came out shaky as what little resolve she had drained out of her.

What had she done?

Samuel kicked the small suitcase and the buckle released, scattering his plain clothing across the floor. Rebecca dropped to her knees and stuffed everything back into the suitcase, the suitcase she had used when she had been a young woman moving into Willard's house. To take over for his dead wife.

What a miserable job she and Willard had done.

Had she actually fallen so far as to compare her parenting skills to her husband's? A murderer?

Rebecca looked up from a kneeling position on the floor.

She had to remain strong.

"It's not forever," she whispered.

She struggled to her feet, then took a step toward Samuel. He recoiled from her, but she persisted. "I love you, but you need to get away for a little bit. Away from this mess until we figure out what's really going on."

"I already confessed." Samuel bowed his head. "You can't lose this land for my stupidity."

"I don't believe for a minute that you're responsible for planting the marijuana plants. Your only mistake was giving your friends, Uri and Jonas, the benefit of the doubt. I talked to the sheriff. Special arrangements have been made with the courts to allow you to travel as long as we assure them you'll come back when the trial starts."

An uneasy feeling roiled in her gut. Courts, lawyers, law enforcement were all contrary to the Amish culture, but there was no way she was going to let Samuel fend for himself in the *English* world.

Willard would have kicked him out and not lost a night's

sleep. She wasn't Willard. She had to protect Samuel. Save him from prison.

A dark memory seeped into her bones.

Willard had been *killed* in prison.

Samuel's rigid posture slackened. He lifted his hands in a supplicating gesture. "Please, *Mem*, don't send me away. I need to be here. To protect you."

Rebecca shook her head slowly, tears forming. "Mr. Yoder has assured me he will make sure his sons stay obedient."

Samuel let out a heavy sigh, as if suggesting Mr. Yoder hadn't had success controlling his sons in the past. Just then, a beeping sounded from the driveway.

"That's your ride. You've met my friend from the diner, Flo. Her son will drive you to the bus depot."

Samuel turned to march up the stairs and Rebecca stood in front of him. "*Neh*. You must leave without any of your electronic things." She closed her eyes briefly, the hollowness expanding inside her. "Please, don't make it harder than it has to be."

Samuel glared at her. He bent over at the waist and scooped up the suitcase, turned and stormed out of the house.

With a hand to her midsection, Rebecca moved to the window and watched Samuel climb into the pickup truck. She stood at the window long after the tailgate disappeared down the country road.

An ache twisted in her heart. She had lost Samuel. Her worst nightmare had come true.

After Samuel had left, the bishop saw to it that some Amish neighbors came over to help her harvest the remaining crops. Perhaps the Fisher family was one step closer to bridging the gap. Rebecca just prayed Samuel's innocence would be proven in court.

A few long days in the fields and they were done for another season. She was relieved they had finished when they had because a storm front moved in, leaving little Apple Creek under dark clouds and steady rain.

And that was fine with Rebecca. It suited her mood.

Rebecca had worked at the diner today and was happy for the distraction. Working on the farm without Samuel only emphasized his absence. But now, after her diner shift, she was tired and wanted to go home and spend time with her daughters.

But first, Rebecca had to run to the local market to grab milk and a few other basics. Groceries in one hand, she fumbled with the handle of the umbrella as the automatic doors swooshed open. The steady rain pelted her umbrella. With the handle of her tote wrapped around her wrist, she reached up and gathered the collar of her coat. She wished the rain could wash away her feelings of indecision.

Of failure…

The swoosh of a tire in a puddle made her instinctively move closer to the buildings. It wouldn't be unheard of for one of the college students to make sport of splashing pedestrians.

Score extra points for soaking the Amish.

She shook her head and kept walking across the small parking lot toward Main Street, her mind otherwise pre-occupied. She was headed back to the diner to meet her ride. Flo had offered to drive her home so she didn't have to spend part of her paltry wages on a ride. She'd have to make some big changes soon. Under the circumstances, she didn't know how much longer she could run the farm, hold down a job at the diner and support her daughters.

"Rebecca."

She stopped in her tracks and turned slowly to face the familiar voice. The professor had pulled his truck up alongside her and had rolled down the passenger window.

"Come on, I'll give you a ride."

Rebecca pointed at the diner. "Flo's going to drive me home. Thanks anyway." The memory of Samuel climbing into the truck and departing for Rochester amplified the emptiness inside her. All her efforts had to mean something. Now she had to do her part, too. Behave like a good Amish woman if she hoped to further patch the tear in her association with the Amish.

"Good night." Rebecca gave her best polite smile, hoping he'd take the hint. She had a lot on her mind, but she hadn't yet figured out how to share it with the professor. She thought she'd have more time.

He reached across the cab of the truck and pushed open the door. "Come in out of the rain. I'll drive you home."

Rebecca slowly walked toward the door, unable to resist his friendly smile. She muttered something under her breath about his smile. This was not unfolding in the way she had intended.

"I don't want Flo to worry."

He pulled out his phone and held it up. "I'll call the diner. Let her know."

When she angled her head with indecision, he said, "You'll save her a trip." He waved his hand in a come-on gesture and she let out a long sigh before closing her umbrella and climbing into the truck. She rested the wet umbrella against the seat while the professor made a quick phone call.

"Are you okay?" he asked, compassion in his tone.

"Um, yeah…" A slow ticking started in her head. She wasn't ready for this conversation.

"It had to be tough to see Samuel leave."

And there it was. The conversation she was dreading. Not because she was still reeling from Samuel's departure, but because there was something else she had to do.

Rebecca bowed her head and played with the straps of her tote at her feet.

"Rebecca," he said softly, "don't be hard on yourself."

Tears started to build and she feared if she opened up to him she'd crumble with all the emotions she had kept locked inside. She wrapped her hand around the door release but stopped when a lightning bolt exploded nearby.

The professor touched the crook of her arm. "I'll just drive you home. We don't have to talk about Samuel."

She met his compassionate gaze. "I should have at the very least thanked you for posting bail and for working within the English system to allow him to travel. I understand that's not always allowed."

"I promised I'd help you."

"Well, I've known men not to keep their promises."

"I'd like the opportunity to show you that some men keep their word."

Rebecca tracked a raindrop as it raced down the window in a wild zigzag, much like her thoughts.

The professor pulled out onto the road. "I'm free this weekend to help you with the harvest again."

Rebecca twisted the handles of her tote bag. "Some neighbors have already helped me. You've done more than enough for my family." She hadn't meant to sound so accusatory. She turned to smile at him in apology.

The professor rubbed his jaw and kept his eyes on the road. The worn wipers scraped across the windshield. *Screech-swoosh-screech-swoosh.*

"I enjoyed working the land." There was a faraway quality to his voice. "I guess it's in my blood."

"You learned very quickly." She remembered his easy

smile as she'd instructed him on how to operate the farming equipment. Not only was he eager to learn, but he also had asked all the right questions.

"I *be* a college graduate."

She frowned, his joke having fallen flat.

Rebecca fingered the strap of her seat belt. "I appreciated your help, but I need to rely on the Amish. I need to be a better example for Samuel and for my daughters." She turned and stared out the window, watching the scenery change outside. Heat pumped out of the vents in the dash and she was grateful she wasn't in a buggy or still out in the rain.

"Well, I'm glad you finally got the help you needed." He sounded hurt, but she had to stick with what she felt was best for her family.

"I should have never gone to an outsider. It's not our way. I should have relied on our community."

The professor slowed at a stop sign and glanced over at her. A muscle ticked in his jaw. With the rain pelting his truck, she felt as if they were all alone. In a cocoon. As if there was no one else in the world.

He reached over and placed his hand over hers. Warm. Protective. Gentle. Qualities she had never seen in her deceased husband. She resisted the urge to pull her hand away. She needed to put distance between them. At the same time, she wanted to savor this connection with the professor one last time.

He brushed his thumb across the back of her hand. "You did nothing wrong by reaching out to me. I've done a lot of research on the *youngie* here. I've gotten to know your son. You weren't wrong in thinking I'd know something that could help you."

"But you didn't. These young men have been doing

things and hiding things right under our noses. I should have been harder on Samuel a long time ago."

"You think he'll be better off away from here?"

"He needs to be away from his gang."

The professor nodded. He lifted his hand and touched her cheek briefly. "Don't push me away, too."

A car honked behind them and the professor dropped his hand and turned his attention to the road.

"I have to," she whispered, her voice barely audible over the noisy wipers. "I have to."

Jake's truck bobbled over the puddle-filled ruts in Rebecca's driveway. The rain pelted the roof of his truck, filling the silence with a steady drumming beat.

"When Samuel comes home for the trial, I hope you make him feel welcome. He needs you now more than ever," Jake said.

Rebecca's bonnet was damp from the rain. The look on her face pained him. "You think I was wrong in sending him away." He was surprised by the harshness of her tone. "I'm not the King family. I didn't throw him out on the street, leaving him to fend for himself. I sent him to an Amish home." She drew in a shaky breath and continued, "I can't have all these *worldly* influences around my young daughters." She tucked a stray hair behind her ear and bowed her head. Her cheeks flared pink from the heater vents. He adjusted the knob to moderate the heat.

"I didn't mean to add to your pain." He rubbed his jaw. "I played a part in Elmer getting kicked out of his home. I encouraged him to share his troubles with his father. His father responded by kicking him out of the house."

"And you feel that led to his car accident?"

"Yes." Jake's gut tightened, remembering the fury Mr. King had unleashed on his son. His father hadn't been understanding and had kicked his struggling son out of the house. Before Jake had had a chance to defuse the situation, given Elmer hope for the future, the young man had revolted and gone on a drinking and drugging binge.

Guilt welled up inside him again. He ran a hand across his forehead, realizing guilt was one of his primary driving forces. It was a horrible way to go through life.

"I'm sure Samuel will be fine," he said, his voice softening.

"I'm doing the best I can to protect my family. My *entire* family."

Did Rebecca think Samuel was guilty? That she had to keep him away from her daughters?

"I wished I could have done more to help you."

"You have. You really have, but I need to learn to rely on my own community. It may or may not be too late for Samuel, but I can't allow him to get away with doing all sorts of worldly things." The lines around her eyes grew tense. "Soon Samuel's case will come to court. Hopefully then we can put this all behind us."

She wrung her hands. "I'm really sorry, Jake."

"Jake? You called me Jake." He couldn't help but smile.

A deep line marred her forehead in confusion.

"You've always called me Professor." He laughed. "Now you finally call me by my given name at the same time that you're brushing me off."

"Brushing you off?" She repeated his words as if she was trying them out, unsure of what they meant. She bowed her head. "I'm sorry. I should have never let you think you could court me."

Jake reached out to touch her cheek, but he pulled his hand back. "Can we still be friends?" He hoped her insular childhood wouldn't allow her to recognize how cliché his comment was.

She pulled the door handle and the dome light clicked on. He studied her. "Can we?"

Rebecca shook her bonneted head. "It would be better if we didn't. I will never leave the Amish and you're not Amish."

"You don't have any non-Amish friends?"

Their gazes lingered. "We aren't friends."

Her words took the wind out of him. "So," he said, his voice hard-edged, "that's it? I don't get a say in this?"

She lifted her brown eyes and stared at him. "We're from two different worlds. It would never work. I could never be happy anywhere but here on the farm."

"Work on the farm is peaceful."

She glanced at him, confused, and suddenly Jake felt as though he wasn't being fair to Rebecca. She was struggling; she didn't need him muddying the waters.

"Give it some time. Wait until Samuel's situation is settled. Don't just…" He let out a long breath. "Don't throw this away."

Rebecca pulled the door closed and the dome light faded to black. She turned to him, her features cast in darkness. "You of all people know how hard it would be for some Amish to leave."

The silence stretched between them as his mother's forlorn face came to mind. Rebecca pushed open the door again and the light revealed a sad smile on her beautiful face.

Jake cupped her cheek. Slowly, she wrapped her fingers around his wrist and pulled his hand away. "Good night, Jake."

He sat back in his seat and watched her run through the rain toward the house, not bothering to stop to open her umbrella. Her tote swung by her side. Once she was inside, a light came on and her shadow paused in front of the window and then disappeared.

He put the car in Reverse and backed out of Rebecca Fisher's driveway.

And out of her life.

TWELVE

"The Amish have moved into New York as land has become more expensive in parts of Ohio and Pennsylvania." Jake paced in front of his Intro to the Amish class. He stopped and scanned the students, mostly composed of freshman and sophomores. He'd never get used to staring at the tops of heads hunched over their laptops, recording his every word. "Others moved here because they had disagreements within their communities."

Or perhaps if they weren't documenting his every word, they were updating their status on whatever social media was popular at the moment with the college set.

He continued, "Many Amish are moving away from farming and into other areas to make a living. They work at local factories or businesses, and some hop into vans and are taken to new neighborhoods to build homes."

As he went on speaking on the subject he knew so well, his mind wandered to the glorious fall afternoon he'd worked on the farm, enjoying every minute with Rebecca.

Jake's heart thudded dully in his chest. Rebecca's request to keep his distance still stung. But it was a request he had to honor.

A young man's hand shot up near the middle of the lecture hall. Jake flattened his palms on the large black marble surface of the long table in the front of the room. "Yes?"

"How come I see all these young Amish guys driving around in cars? Are the buggies simply for show?"

Jake put the cap on the dry erase marker and twisted it. "We'll be talking more about Rumspringa and the youth in the Amish next week. But in short, no, the buggies are not for show. The Amish in this community—the baptized Amish—do not drive cars."

"But they can ride in cars?" A young girl in front with her chin resting on her palm scrunched up her nose.

"Right." Jake glanced at his watch, trying not to show his frustration. "Are you guys also reading the text? It might help you retain some of the information we've gone over in class. You're in college now, so you need to step up your study skills. You're all registered for or have had Study Skills 101, right?"

He heard a few groans and laughed. Not many of these kids appreciated their education and probably thought nothing of the Amish not being allowed to attend school past the eighth grade.

Class was winding down. "Okay, be sure to turn in your papers by 5:00 p.m. tomorrow online. Or if you have them now, I'll take them."

Jake closed his laptop and Tommy approached his desk as the students filed out. "When do you need the papers graded?" Tommy graded the shorter papers and Jake graded the term-length project and their final.

"Next Monday would be great."

Tommy made a noise of dissatisfaction.

"Too much work for you?"

Tommy shook his head. "Not at all."

"If you're unsure, I'll spot-check a few to make sure you're on the right track."

Tommy nodded.

"You finish your applications for grad school?"

"Working on it." The young man drummed his fingers on the table.

"Is something wrong?"

"Nothing I can't work out."

And Jake didn't doubt it. Tommy had left his Amish home at eighteen and worked his way to a GED and then college. He was nothing if not resourceful.

"How's your senior project going?" Jake asked.

"The King family isn't thrilled with me coming around. Samuel and I are friends." He shrugged. "Guilty by association." He lifted his eyebrows. "Jonas and Uri were key to some of my research." Tommy seemed uncharacteristically glum. He was usually pretty easygoing.

"Reach out to other *youngie*. You can be resourceful."

"Perhaps."

"Things will calm down."

"It usually does." Something dark fluttered in the depths of Tommy's eyes. "How's Mrs. Fisher doing? All this had to come as a blow on the heels of the tragedy with her husband."

"Yes, it has." Jake purposely kept his answer short, not wanting Tommy to know that Jake had crossed the professional line with Rebecca. But that was all in the past.

Tommy frowned. "Sounds like we've both alienated the local Amish. It doesn't bode well for our respective futures."

"Did you hear Samuel left town?"

Tommy arched an eyebrow but didn't acknowledge what he knew.

"Rebecca sent him to live in an Amish community near Rochester. For now."

Tommy tucked his laptop under his arm. "I better start cultivating more Amish friendships."

"Why don't you find some who are a little less worldly? It might give you a different perspective. Some *youngie* actually try to follow the rules."

Tommy rolled his eyes. "What fun would that be, dude? I'd have to tag along on the farm or at those tone-deaf singings for the goody-goodies. Remember, I've already experienced that firsthand."

Jake clapped his teaching assistant's shoulder with the palm of his hand. "Don't let anyone ever tell you that you haven't acclimated to the outside world, *dude*." Jake smiled when he emphasized Tommy's favorite word.

"I am nothing if not adaptable. My life experience up to now has taught me that."

"With your background, your senior project will have a unique perspective. Keep plugging away. Don't let this setback throw you."

Tommy's cell phone dinged and he glanced down at the screen. "Gotta run. I have some things to take care of."

"Night. Contact me if you have any questions once the term papers start coming in."

"Sounds good." Tommy stuffed his laptop into his backpack and hiked the strap up on his shoulder.

"You got your laptop fixed?"

"Yes. Couldn't live without one."

Jake watched the young man stomp up the stairs of the large lecture hall and disappear through the back exit. Was Tommy happy? Could people make huge life changes and not have regrets?

His parents were an example that it couldn't be done.

Could Jake be any different?

* * *

After his class ended, Jake decided to drive out to Bishop Lapp's home. When he arrived, he double-checked the time. The dark rain clouds hovering in the distance made it seem later than it was.

Jake climbed out of the truck and strolled to where he'd noticed an older Amish man leading a horse into the barn.

"How can I help you, Professor Burke?" Bishop Lapp asked without looking at him. The elderly gentleman hiked the leather straps from the horse's rigging onto a hook; his arms shook under the weight. Jake stepped forward, ready to help the man, when something made him stop. Perhaps it was the quick sideways look the bishop shot at him. Perhaps an offer of help would be offensive to a man who had spent his life on a farm.

Or perhaps an offer of help from an outsider was unwanted.

Bishop Lapp limped to the back wall and grabbed his cane. He leaned on it, resting one hand on top of the other. "Looking for more information for your study of the Plain people?" His even tone made it difficult for Jake to understand the elderly man's frame of mind.

"Actually, no."

The bishop lifted his chin in understanding. "My son Lester told me you were asking about joining the Amish. Do you think coming to me will yield you different answers?"

"I'm knowledgeable about the Amish. I understand the difficulties of joining the community as an outsider."

"Understanding the difficulties on an intellectual level is different—" the bishop enunciated each word as if to emphasize his point "—than becoming a humble man who lives in a community as a baptized member."

Jake ran a hand across his jaw. "I love Rebecca Fisher."

Did he really say that out loud?

The bishop leaned heavily on his cane and met his gaze. "Your *dat* loved your *mem*?"

"You knew my parents? You know who I am?" His father had changed their last name once they'd left Apple Creek to further distance themselves from their Amish background.

"Your parents were Mary Miller and John Leising, right?"

"Yes." A muscle ticked in his jaw. "How did you know? I've told very few people."

"You have your *mem*'s eyes. But I didn't know for sure until now."

"So, you knew them?"

"I wasn't bishop then, but yes, I knew them. Your mother was a fine woman and your father had a taste for the worldly." The older man pressed his lips together. "How are they?"

Jake glanced down, then back up at the bishop. "They're deceased."

The bishop ran a hand down his unkempt beard. "I'm sorry. Too young."

Nostalgia twisted Jake's insides as long-forgotten memories of his parents crossed his mind.

"But I suppose I remember them as the youth they were."

"My mother did die young. I was only ten. My father died when I was seventeen."

The bishop cleared his throat, as if the subject was too uncomfortable. "Now you believe you want to return to your Amish roots?"

"I have been thinking about it for a long time now. Even before I met Rebecca." The peace he felt in her presence, on her farm, had made the feelings he had buried come to the surface. "I have to continue to pray on it."

"Come with me." The bishop limped with his cane toward the barn door. "I have some information regarding baptismal classes in the house."

Jake followed him and waited outside on the porch for the older gentleman to return. When he did, the bishop handed him a book.

"Whatever you decide, you cannot make this decision lightly."

Yet another rainy day saturated the fields in Apple Creek. Rebecca was beginning to wonder if it was ever going to let up. She sat in the rocker while enjoying a cup of tea and watched Katie and Grace, a luxurious break she rarely afforded herself.

A rumble of thunder rolled over the house and a chill skittered down her spine. Rebecca grabbed two small quilts off the wood stand and put one on each girl's lap. Katie was reading a Laura Ingalls Wilder book to her little sister. "Are you girls okay?"

Katie put her finger on the page to mark her spot and looked up.

"The storm doesn't bother you, does it?"

They shook their heads in unison. "There's no reason to be afraid," Katie said, sounding older than her eight years. "We're all snug like bugs in our house. Do you know we have a house like in *Little House on the Prairie*?"

A smile tugged at the corners of Rebecca's mouth. She had loved those books and had feared she might never be able to share them with her girls because Willard had been against most every book. She shook away the thought, unwilling to let the past ruin their cozy afternoon.

Another thunderclap rocked the house.

Rebecca looked up at the ceiling and frowned. "Buttercup's not a fan of storms." Her gaze dropped to her daughters snuggled up in the corner of the room. "I'm going to run out to the barn and make sure she's okay. You girls keep reading your book."

"Can I go with you? I can give her carrots." Grace jumped up, the quilt pooling around her feet.

"Oh, but it's yucky out. Why don't you stay inside with your big sister? Keep each other company."

With a huff, Grace plopped down on the rocker her mother had vacated. Rebecca picked up the quilt and tucked it around her daughter, ignoring her little tantrum. "I'll be back in soon and then I'll warm up some soup for dinner. Okay?"

Rebecca put on her raincoat, flipped up the hood and grabbed a few carrots to put in her pocket. She opened the back door and hustled down the back steps. Her boots squished in the mud as she crossed the yard to the barn.

When will this rain ever stop?

Squinting against the pelting rain, she picked up speed. She clutched her hood to prevent a gust of wind from blowing it down.

When she reached the barn and pushed back the door, another rumble of thunder rolled across the sky. Goose bumps prickled her skin. Sensing someone was watching her, she glanced behind her. Nothing but fields.

A truck barreled down the country road.

Turning her attention back to the task at hand, she entered the dimly lit barn and pulled a carrot out of her pocket.

"Hey, Buttercup. Everything's okay," she said in a soothing voice. "The storm will pass quickly." A part of her felt as if she was trying to convince herself.

The storm in her life would pass quickly. Reaching

through the wide spaces in the bars of the stall, she patted the horse. Buttercup neighed. "You've been through a lot, too, huh?"

Buttercup eagerly ate the carrot and then sniffed Rebecca's hand, eager for more. She reached into her pocket and found another carrot. "Here you go."

She rubbed the side of the horse's head until she seemed to calm down. She decided to find a blanket for Buttercup, to comfort her.

She walked to the back of the barn and past a door yawning open to the back fields. Something blue flashed in her periphery and then disappeared behind the outbuilding where Willard had kept a stash of weapons. She often wondered what he had been planning if he hadn't been caught. She hadn't been in the building since before Willard's arrest.

Biting her lower lip, she wondered if she had imagined the movement.

She returned to Buttercup, covered her with a blanket and patted her. "Everything is going to be okay."

Rebecca grabbed the pitchfork and measured the weight of it in her hands. With a fluttery feeling in her chest, she strode out of the barn, glancing toward the house. Her daughters were in there. They were safe. She'd never be able to relax unless she checked the outbuilding and made sure someone wasn't trespassing on her property.

Pulling her hood back over her head, she held her raincoat close at her neck and gripped the pitchfork tightly in the other hand. She'd never be able to use it as a weapon, but what the potential trespasser didn't know might save her.

A long time ago, she had ceased being a quiet Amish wife. She had to be the head of this household. Protect her family.

You're seeing things, silly woman. Willard's voice clashed with the wind and rain and a dull roar of thunder moving off to the east.

Each step seemed harder to take, but she knew if she stopped she'd lose her nerve. When she reached the outbuilding, she pressed her body against the wall and peered toward the open door.

Was someone in there?

A rustle of plastic sounded overhead. She glanced up just in time to see a huge blue tarp dropping out of the sky. She raised her hands to fling it away when something heavy landed on top of her, shoving her down into the wet mud. Her pitchfork useless by her side.

Dear Lord, help me.

THIRTEEN

Jake placed the book on the passenger seat of his truck and made a spontaneous decision to drive over to check on Rebecca and the girls. He knew the bishop had seen to it that she had some help with the farm now that Uri and Jonas were prohibited from working for her. But there were always things to be done.

He knew Rebecca wanted him to stay away because their future was predetermined due to their different backgrounds. He tapped the book on the seat next to him. Nervous indecision pressed on his chest. Maybe…just maybe he could change that.

As Jake rounded the curve on the country road, the clouds had turned an ominous steely gray. He adjusted the windshield wiper speed to keep pace with the driving rain. A rumble of thunder sounded overhead. When he turned up Rebecca's driveway, her quaint home came into view beyond his blurry windshield. He really needed to replace his wipers.

Jake climbed out of the vehicle, flipped up his hood and shuddered against the cool rain. Bent forward, he jogged toward the house. He lifted his hand to knock when he heard a cry in the distance. He spun around and squinted toward the sound. Katie and Grace were holding hands, dodging mud puddles and running toward the barn.

Unease twisted around his spine.

Where was their mother?

Perhaps she had been in front of the girls and had reached the barn before the strange muffled cry rang out. *What was that?* Not wanting to waste another moment, he ran after them, muttering his annoyance when his dress shoes sank in the mud with each step.

He also really needed to get some boots.

He caught up with the girls inside the barn's entrance. Katie had her arm around Grace, comforting her. He glanced around the barn. *No Rebecca.*

"Girls, what are you doing out in this weather? Your mother will be worried about you."

The girls turned around as a unit. Grace had red-rimmed eyes and wet cheeks, both from the rain and tears. His heart stuttered.

"What's wrong?"

"*Mem* came out to the barn to check on Buttercup and—" Katie sniffed "—and she didn't come back." Katie squeezed her sister's shoulders. "I thought she couldn't get Buttercup to settle down and that's why it was taking a long time." The corners of her mouth tugged down in a heartbreaking display of emotion. "She's gone."

Tamping down his growing unease, Jake crouched down to the girls' level. "Are you sure she's not in the house?"

"*Neh*, we came from the house."

Grace's big eyes canvased the barn. "She's missing. Maybe she's gone like our big brother."

Jake gently touched Grace's arm. "Your *mem* wouldn't leave you."

"After our *dat* went away," Katie joined in, "Samuel promised us he would never leave. But he did."

A knot formed in Jake's stomach. These poor children had experienced much loss in their young lives.

Jake surreptitiously scanned the barn behind the girls, looking for any signs of mischief. "Your *mem* came out here to check on Buttercup?"

Grace nodded and her chest rose and fell on a sob. "Buttercup doesn't like thunder."

As if on cue, the horse neighed her annoyance at a distant rumble of thunder. Jake strolled over to the horse's stall with the girls and let them pet her. "Buttercup's fine."

His pulse ticked in his ears, like time slipping away. But he didn't want to jump to conclusions or to alarm the girls. "Let me get you both inside, then I'll come back out and find your mom."

"Where can *Mem* be?" Katie asked. The slightly older girl easily slipped into the role of big sister, protector. But even she had a hitch in her voice.

Grace broke away from her big sister and clung to Jake. He wrapped an arm around her and squeezed. "It's going to be okay." A drip of rain plopped down onto her bonnet from a leak in the barn roof. He smiled, trying to lighten the mood. "Let's get you inside where it's dry."

Grace took his hand. The feel of the little girl's cool hand in his caught him off guard. His parents had never been affectionate. It was not a common trait of the Amish. Yet Grace must have been frightened enough to reach up and take his hand. He smiled down and gently squeezed her hand. "Everything will be okay."

Grace nodded.

Katie marched ahead and when they stepped outside the barn, he noticed the rain had turned from a torrential downpour to a gentle shower. In the distance against the gunmetal sky, a streak of lightning flashed. He noticed

Katie quietly counting under her breath. Then a crash of thunder. Grace startled next to him.

"Seven," Katie said confidently. "The storm is seven miles away. We're okay."

Jake reached out with his free hand and gently touched Katie's shoulder. "Yes, we are. Let's hurry inside so you don't get too wet."

They pounded up the steps of the porch. The front door stood open and, instinctively, Jake moved the girls behind him.

"Did you girls leave the door open?"

Grace shrugged and Katie looked a little sheepish.

Jake stepped into the room, holding the girls back. He called out for Rebecca, but he was met with only the soft sound of rain on the roof.

"No, Professor, she's outside. I told you," Katie said, her voice edged with youthful exasperation.

"I know, honey. The door was open. I wanted to make sure she hadn't returned while we were in the barn."

Jake made the girls sit in the rockers in the front room while he quickly checked all the rooms in the house, calling Rebecca's name while he did.

As the seconds ticked away, his unease amped up.

Something was wrong.

"Katie, follow me to the door." When she did, he turned and said, "Lock it behind me. I'll be right back with your *mem*."

She nodded. Jake paused on the porch while he listened for the snap of the bolt. He pulled his hood up, stood at the edge of the porch and scanned the yard.

"Rebecca," he called, cupping his mouth. "Rebecca."

His mouth grew dry.

No answer.

The wind kicked up and blew leaves across the yard,

some settling against the grate protecting the underside of the porch.

Jake stepped off the porch and ran toward the barn.

Where are you, Rebecca? Where are you?

Planting her palms into the cold, wet mud, Rebecca pushed herself up. The blue tarp crinkled in the wind and the distinct smell of plastic mixed with the earthy scent of mud tickled her nose. She braced herself, fearing whoever had thrown this down over her would jump on top of her to finish her off.

Fear tingled her scalp.

Maybe the wind had blown the tarp down on her. Maybe her imagination was getting the best of her.

Yet the tarp felt weighted at the corners.

Pulse whooshing in her ears, she held out her arm and yanked back a side of the stiff tarp, finally untangling herself from this mess. A cool breeze caressed her damp cheeks as she squinted up at the darkening sky. The shadow of the outbuilding hunkered over her like an ominous threat.

"Is someone there?" Her soft voice shook, barely audible over the stiff winds.

A solid thud and a groan sounded from around the back of the building. Gathering the folds of her dress, she pushed to her feet. She picked up the pitchfork. Pressing against the rough wood of the poorly cared for shed, she shuffled toward the edge, afraid of being detected.

Someone was running across the field. Away from her.

She stood paralyzed, flat against the building. Her grip tightened on the tool.

Was it one of the Yoder brothers?

She couldn't be sure. All she could see was a dark form growing smaller across the field.

A deep voice carried on the wind. Was someone calling her?

"Rebecca."

Glancing toward the barn, she realized the house was out of view, but at least whoever had thrown the tarp on her was running away from the house.

Her girls should be safe.

A tingling started in her fingers and worked its way up her arms. She had to check on them to be sure.

As she stepped away from the shed, she noticed its door yawned open. All her senses went on high alert. The glass on the bottom pane closest to the door handle was broken.

Willard used to keep the outbuilding's door locked. The building was little more than an oversize shed. He'd kept weapons in there. A million memories swirled in her head. Willard's angry voice to stay away from his stuff scraped across her brain.

Willard's gone. He can't hurt me.

Holding her breath, Rebecca pushed the door all the way open. It creaked on its hinges and bounced off a nearby table. Goose bumps raced across her flesh as she stepped into the small structure. The unkempt ten-by-ten space was empty save for branches hanging from the ceiling.

The marijuana? She reached up and touched the drying leaves. A pain started behind her eyes.

How could this be?

Rebecca lifted her hand to her temples and rubbed.

"Rebecca!" The familiar sound of Jake's voice made her spin around.

"I'm here." She ran toward the door and tripped on the lip of the doorway. She caught herself on the doorframe.

Jake came into view and the look of relief on his face caught her off guard and secretly thrilled her. He gripped her shoulders and angled his head. "What happened to you?" He stared at the pitchfork.

Rebecca leaned it against the wall.

"I'm fine. I'm fine." She searched frantically behind him, looking toward the main house. "Are the girls okay?"

"Yes, yes. They're fine. I saw them before I came looking for you. Now tell me. What happened?"

Rebecca pointed up, to the roof of the outbuilding. "Someone threw a tarp down on me. And then he took off. Over there." She pointed across the field.

Jake squinted in the direction she pointed. "I don't see anyone."

"I'm afraid he's gotten away."

Jake turned his attention back to Rebecca. He brushed his thumb across her cheek. When his thumb came away with dirt, she stepped back and swiped at her face, heat reddening her cheeks. "I landed face-first in the dirt."

"Are you okay?"

She stepped out of the doorway and raised her palm to the contents inside. "Look at this. Tell me what this means."

Jake slipped past her and took in the scene.

"I thought the police destroyed the drugs," she whispered.

"Whoever knocked you out must have grabbed a few plants before they escaped."

"Why are they hanging the plants?"

"I don't know much about marijuana, but I imagine they needed to dry it out and cure it. To get it ready to sell." Jake touched one of the leaves. "It seems too damp in here."

"They probably were trying to put the tarp on the roof to stop it from leaking." A smile pulled at the corners of her mouth.

He smiled, mirroring her, but one of his brows pulled

down at the corner as if her sudden change in mood had confused him. He wiped what she suspected was another spot of mud from her cheek. "You are a mysterious woman, Rebecca. Why are you smiling?"

"Don't you see? This—" she held her palm up to the shed that had seen better days "—this proves my son is innocent. Samuel's near Rochester. He couldn't have been responsible for this. He's innocent."

FOURTEEN

The hope in Rebecca's eyes crushed Jake. He wanted nothing more than to reassure her. To tell her that Samuel *was* innocent.

What did this incident really mean? Leaning over, he dragged the damp tarp away from the building and saw nothing other than an uneven muddy patch. He held out his hand to the dirt staining the front of her dress. "This is where you fell?"

Rebecca brushed at her dress but it only served to rub it in. "Yes. I didn't see the man until he was running away." A look of disgust flickered across her face. Jake turned and squinted up at the roof of the small outbuilding.

A gust of wind whipped up and brought with it more rain.

"Let's get inside." With a hand gently on the small of her back, Jake guided Rebecca across the uneven earth.

When they reached the house, Rebecca turned the handle and found the door locked. A look of concern creased her smooth forehead.

"I told them to lock it."

Rebecca looked up at him with gratitude in her eyes. "Thank you for looking out for them. I shouldn't have left them alone, but we were all worried about Buttercup in this storm…"

"They're fine. Don't beat yourself up."

"It's so dark out here. Anyone could be out there." Her lips began to tremble. "We're out here all alone. If something more serious had happened to me, who would have…"

Jake leaned in close and resisted the urge to kiss away the tears. "It'll be okay. You have to trust in God."

"I've done nothing *but* trust in God." She plucked at her skirt again. "Look at me."

Jake stared at the top of her bonnet, unsure of how to comfort her. He didn't want to offend her by drawing her into his arms. He didn't want to add to her inner turmoil.

"Are you ready to go in?" he whispered. He knew she wouldn't want to upset the girls by appearing out of sorts.

Rebecca lifted her head and swiped at her cheeks, leaving more mud streaks. Jake felt a smile tugging on the corners of his mouth. "You are a real mess."

"I'm fine. It's not unusual to get a little dirty working the farm."

"In the rain," he added.

"Exactly." A bright light shone in her eyes. A slow smile crept across his face in response to hers. He had done that. He had brought Rebecca a small moment of happiness.

They locked gazes, and then she lifted her hand and knocked. From inside, he heard a fumbling as someone worked the lock. The door eased open and Katie's curious gaze appeared in the crack. When she saw her mother, she pulled the door all the way open.

"Mem," Katie said, her eyes drawn to her mother's dirty clothes. "What happened to your dress?"

Rebecca waved her hand in dismissal. "I fell in the

mud." When Katie's eyes opened wide, her mother reassured her. "I'm fine. Nothing a good scrub won't get out."

Katie stepped back and Grace ran up, wrapping her arms around her mother's waist undeterred by the mud. "Don't ever leave us."

Jake read every sorrowful emotion playing out on Rebecca's pretty face. Squaring her shoulders, she said, "Oh honey, I was checking on a few things and got caught in the rain." She ran her hand down her daughter's head. "You're getting all muddy." She took her daughter's hands and held her at arm's length. "I'm here. I'm your *mem*. I'm not going anywhere."

Across the room, Katie stared at Jake with her little mouth set in a pout. Then her steely gaze landed on her mother. "You have dirt on your face."

Rebecca lifted her hand to her cheek. "I know. I'll have to clean up."

"When is Samuel coming home? *He* should have been checking on Buttercup."

Rebecca stepped back and Jake caught her arm to steady her, then quickly dropped his hand. Rebecca met Jake's gaze.

"We'll talk about this later," Rebecca said to her daughter.

"*Aenti* Gloria said you sent my brother away because he was bad. Now with him gone things would be better." The child sounded much older than her years.

Rebecca slowly sat down on the rocker, playing with the cold, wet, muddy folds of her skirt. "This is a very grown-up conversation. Your brother made some bad decisions. He didn't follow the rules. We must pray that he finds his way."

Katie's lips twitched and she looked up at Jake. "*He* shouldn't keep coming around here. It's not right."

Both he and Rebecca realized Katie had redirected her fear over her missing mother to disappointment over her brother's absence. When that didn't earn her any satisfaction, she channeled her anger toward Jake.

"I wanted to make sure your mom was okay," Jake said.

Rebecca stood and opened the door. "And since I am, Professor Burke is heading home," she said pointedly to Jake. "Thank you for stopping by, but my girls and I are fine." Her eyes projected an apology.

Jake stepped closer to Rebecca and whispered, "Can we talk on the porch?"

Rebecca sighed heavily.

Without waiting for an answer, Jake slipped the quilt from the rack and draped it around her shoulders. *"Please,"* he whispered.

She seemed to take in the room, then stepped out on the porch with him.

She crossed her arms under the quilt. "What is it?"

"I don't want you to get your hopes up."

Her eye twitched. "About Samuel?"

"Yes, just because he's not here doesn't make him innocent. He could have been working with the Yoder brothers. Or someone else. One of them might have thrown the tarp over you today."

Rebecca bit her lower lip. "Call the sheriff. Tell him what happened here. Ask if he'll check on the Yoders. Maybe one of them will...what would you say...crack? Can you do that for me?"

"Yes." He touched her elbow and she stepped back as if it burned. "You need to be careful out here all alone with the girls."

"This is my home." She set her jaw. "And the more I think of it, you shouldn't be here. It doesn't help. I'm trying desperately to be a good influence on my girls. We need stability."

Bowing his head, Jake ran a hand across the back of his neck. He hadn't anticipated sharing his plans, but he needed to reach across the gap. "I've talked to Bishop Lapp."

"About Samuel?" The indignation was evident in her tone. "I don't need—"

"I talked to him about me," he interrupted.

She looked up, curiosity lighting her brown eyes. *"You?"*

Jake leaned on the porch railing and crossed his arms. "I have never felt more at home than I do here. With you."

Rebecca tugged the quilt closer around her neck. "I don't understand."

"I'm exploring being baptized into the Amish community."

Her brows snapped together. "What? Why?" She leaned toward him, then stepped back, flattening herself against the siding of her house. "Is this all part of your research? For some paper?" Her eyes sparked with anger. "We are not…" She bowed her head and grew quiet.

He pushed off the railing and stood in front of her, careful not to make her feel trapped. "No, it's not for a paper. It's not for my job at the university… It's for you."

His heart pounded in his ears and her face went still. She took a step to the side and yanked open the door. She paused but didn't turn around.

"Despite that fancy education, you have it all wrong about the Amish. All wrong."

She stepped inside and closed the door. He heard the lock click.

"You look exhausted," Flo said, screwing the silver top of the saltshaker back on after refilling it. She placed it in the rack next to the pepper, set it aside, then turned to give her full attention to Rebecca.

"I am. I couldn't sleep." Rebecca blinked her eyes a few times, trying to get rid of the gritty feeling. She grabbed the gray bin of clean silverware and placed it on the counter with a clatter.

Flo laid out a paper napkin and rolled a fork, spoon and steak knife in it. "No need to be lying awake at night. You did the best thing for Samuel right now."

"I have faith Samuel will be okay." Rebecca sounded bleak, unconvincing.

Flo rolled up another napkin with silverware and tossed it into the basket. The older woman tipped her head toward the large bin of silverware. "I've heard busy hands are the best antidote for a worried mind." She arched a brow in amusement.

Rebecca felt her face grow warm. "I'm sorry—I'm distracted." She scooped up a knife, fork and spoon, placed them on a napkin and started rolling. She hated bringing her worries to her friend, but she felt lonely sometimes and she couldn't get the conversation she had had with Jake yesterday out of her mind.

Jake was considering joining the Amish community.

"I have a feeling it's not only Samuel who's distracting you." Flo never missed anything.

"Jake…" She lifted her eyes to meet Flo's. The older woman nodded in understanding.

Rebecca held up her hand to stop her friend before she made a comment that would make her blush. "I have to tell you because you're the only one I can trust not to judge me."

Flo rested her hip against the counter and slipped her hands into her apron. "What is it, honey?"

"Jake told me he's thinking about joining the Amish."

Her pale eyebrows shot up. "Really?"

Rebecca nodded slowly, feeling the world close in on her. Heat gathered around her face and she tugged on the collar of her dress.

"Do people do that? I don't think I've ever heard of an outsider joining the Amish community. I usually hear about the heartache when one of the Amish youth runs away." Flo stood straighter, her eyes unfocused as if lost in thought. "*Can* people do that?"

"It's highly unusual, but it has been done."

A light came into Flo's eyes and she lifted her hands and covered her mouth. "Oh dear, he's doing it so he can be with you, isn't he?"

Rebecca bowed her head and shook it. "He must make the decision on his own for reasons more than me." Her mind flashed back to how comfortable Jake seemed working on the farm. His mention of feeling at peace. She pressed her lips together and sighed. "*Neh*, he can't join the Amish community just because of me."

With her index finger, Flo lifted Rebecca's chin to force her to meet her gaze. "You *are* worth it. Don't underestimate yourself."

Rebecca shook her head again, this time more adamantly. "He should do it because he wants to embrace the Amish ways. No other reason."

"Of course, of course," Flo agreed, "but you would be a nice bonus."

Rebecca was surprised to hear a giggle escape her lips. "You're the best part of this job. I'm grateful for your friendship."

Flo made a dramatic show of looking around the diner. "That's high praise," she said, her words dripping with sarcasm. Then her face grew serious and she pulled Rebecca's hands into hers. "It's time you found happiness."

"It's not the—"

"—Amish way," Flo finished her sentence. "I truly don't think God would mind if you found happiness."

With Flo's words swirling around her head, Rebecca picked up more silverware and set it down on the napkin.

Could she and Jake find happiness together?

The empty space inside her no longer seemed so empty. Dare she hope?

The jangling bell on the door signaled the arrival of a few customers coming in for an early breakfast.

"Have a seat wherever you'd like," Flo hollered to them. The older woman grabbed the coffee carafe. "I'll get this table."

"Thanks." Rebecca's gratitude was short-lived. The sheriff walked through the door with his keen focus solely on her.

Rebecca filled a mug with coffee. Black. Just how the sheriff liked it. He strolled over to the counter and slipped onto the stool in front of the mug. "Morning, Rebecca. Thanks for the coffee."

"Morning, Sheriff Maxwell."

He took a sip, studying her over the rim. "Have you recovered from last night?"

"I'm fine. No worse for the wear, I suppose. But it'll take some work to get the mud out of my dress." She smiled. "Did you have a chance to talk to the Yoder boys?" Butterflies flitted in her stomach as she waited for the sheriff's response.

"Yeah. I met Jake at their house. Mr. Yoder assured us that both boys had been home all day doing chores on the farm. At the approximate time of the incident, Mrs. Yoder said the family was gathered for dinner."

A sinking feeling weighed on Rebecca. "I see."

"There's always a chance they're mistaken," the sheriff

said, setting his spoon on the napkin. A brown spot grew where he had placed it.

"Mr. And Mrs. Yoder are good people. I don't believe they'd lie." Outside the window, the weather was dark and dreary, like her mood.

Flo brushed past her and pinned her order to the wheel above the window leading into the kitchen. "Morning, Sheriff Maxwell. Hungry for some breakfast? Pancakes?"

The sheriff took another sip of his coffee, then pushed away from the counter and stood. "No, thanks. I have to get on the road."

He turned to Rebecca. "Contact me if you need anything. Please." She must have been wearing a look of concern because the sheriff paused. "Hannah would want you to reach out. To me. *To her.* She loves you and doesn't want anything to happen to you."

"Thank you." Rebecca slowly blinked. "Have a good day, Sheriff."

Flo picked up a small stack of plastic menus and pressed them into Rebecca's hands. "Next table's yours."

"Thanks." Rebecca started to walk away when she heard Flo mumble.

"Professor Burke would look great in suspenders and a straw hat."

Rebecca whirled around and playfully whacked her friend with a menu. "Shush."

"You shush." Flo reached out and squeezed Rebecca's hand. "It's time things turned around for you."

"Go ahead, I'll lock up," Rebecca said to Flo at the end of their shift a few days later. She had sent her girls to stay overnight at Mark and Gloria's house. Even though Rebecca hated to have her daughters away at night, she knew playing with their cousins afforded a wonderful distraction. They needed a stable home environment.

Jake's conversation came to mind again. The girls could use a father in their lives. A loving father.

Neh, neh, neh. If Jake decided to become Amish, it had to be for the right reasons.

"No, no, I'll stay and help." Flo dumped the remainder of the coffee down the drain.

"Go." Rebecca scooted in next to her, took the carafe from her hand and set it on the counter. She'd wash it in a minute. "I know you wanted to get home to watch your TV program. Go."

"Ah, you say that like it's a bad thing." Flo tilted her head and gave Rebecca a sad smile. Rebecca didn't know how to respond anymore. It seemed lately everyone watched her with an air of pity. At least when the tourists came to town in full force next summer, she could go back to playing her stereotypical Amish role. She could at least meet someone's expectations.

Met real-live Amish woman. *Check.*

"Are your girls staying with their aunt and uncle again tonight?"

Rebecca wiped the counter down. *"Yah."* Even though she hated to admit it, she felt safer knowing they were with Mark and his family. Until she cleared Samuel's name and found out who was growing marijuana on her farm, things wouldn't feel safe there.

She scrubbed the carafe a little more vigorously than necessary, trying to hold back her emotions.

Flo gestured with her chin toward the last table. "Want me to tell him it's time to pack it in?" she asked in a protective tone. "I don't know why those college kids have to hog our tables to do their schoolwork when there's a perfectly good library on campus, right?"

Rebecca shrugged. She had only been on the local campus once, and after being attacked she didn't plan on going back anytime soon.

"The customer's fine. I'll give him a few more minutes while I clean up."

"As long as you're sure."

Rebecca watched her friend remove her apron, drape it over her arm and slip out the front door, the bells clacking on the glass.

Rebecca organized things to make startup easier for the first shift. She glanced up and the young man was still sitting there, his back to her, she supposed, to gain a better view out the window.

She flicked off a few lights, figuring he'd take a hint without her having to ask him to leave. Confrontation had never been her strong suit. She tidied up a few more things, then peeked into the dining room through the service window. The young man was no longer sitting in the corner booth. A hint of relief swept through her. Problem solved.

Rebecca strode to the front door and turned the key in the lock. She paused a minute and stared over the darkened street. Her haunted expression stared back at her. Would her life ever calm down? Would she ever find the peace she once enjoyed living on an Amish farm? *Before* she'd married Willard. She longed for it, but she knew she had to be humble and trust in God's plan.

She set the keys on the edge of the counter when she realized she'd forgotten to empty the orange-handled decaf carafe sitting on the warmer in the far corner.

A scraping sound—the sound of someone dragging keys across the counter—made her swing around. Her heart stopped at the strange expression on the young man's face.

"Hello, Mrs. Fisher."

"Hello…Tommy." *Jake's assistant.* Her gaze dropped to the keys in his hand. *Her keys.* "I didn't realize you were still here." She lifted a shaky hand to the corner booth. "I didn't realize that was you in the booth."

"I was in the little boy's room."

She held her hand out for her keys. "I'll let you out."

Tommy pressed the keys between his palms and pulled them close to his chest. "You want me to leave?" His mocking tone sent terror racing through her veins.

"Um, yes…" She drew her elbows in close to her sides. *It's Tommy. Jake's assistant. He's harmless.* Dread tightened like a band around her lungs. "We're closed for the night," she said, a little more forcefully.

Tommy pivoted to look out the front window, then turned back to her, a brazen expression on his face. "Shame. I have more studying to do."

"Where are your books?"

He gestured with his head toward a backpack resting on the floor near a booth.

"I'm sorry. The diner is closed." Rebecca clasped her hands in front of her as she struggled to rein in her frantic emotions. Something was off.

"I know." Tommy made no effort to move toward the front door. "I'm not ready to leave." He tossed the keys from one hand to the other; each time they landed in his hand with a loud jangle of metal.

Rebecca wiped her sweat-slicked palms on her cotton skirt. She held out her hand again, determined to be more forceful. "I need my keys, *please.*"

An oily smile slid across Tommy's lips and he made no effort to offer her the keys.

Rebecca forced a shaky smile, trying to hide her nerves. "I need the keys to unlock the door to let you out."

Tommy lifted the keys and tossed them well past her.

Rebecca spun round. The keys crashed into a framed football jersey from a long-ago high school state championship team and clunked onto the ground.

The words *why are you doing this?* froze on her lips as a cold chill swept over every inch of her skin.

Rebecca ran around the counter to put a barrier between her and Tommy. She glanced over her shoulder to the kitchen, but the back door to the alley was locked and she needed the key to unlock it. Same went for the front door.

Tommy slowly walked toward her. "I have good news and I have bad news. Which would you like first?"

Rebecca shook her head in disbelief. "You need to leave. I have to close the diner," she repeated.

"Okay, I'll give you the good news." He dragged his hand across his mussed hair. "Samuel was telling the truth. He wasn't involved with the drugs at all." A light lit his eyes in a way that sent terror pumping through her veins. "*I* was the one who recruited your Amish farmhands into helping me grow marijuana on your land."

Rebecca stared at Tommy in disbelief, her vision narrowing and tiny dots dancing in her eyes.

"Don't you want to know the bad news?" His lips thinned into a line and he shook his head slowly. "You won't be able to tell anyone because I'm going to kill you."

FIFTEEN

Jake walked across campus to grab a bite to eat before heading home. The school kept the student union open late for hungry students. A half carton of expired milk and a mushy cucumber were probably the only things waiting for him in his refrigerator at home.

When Jake reached the student union, he noticed the news station blaring on the wall TV. He slowed when he saw the news truck on a country road in front of a familiar home.

The laughter of students at a nearby table dulled to a distant din. He moved closer to the television. Jake glanced around the mostly empty dining room. No one except the young woman reading a novel bothered to look up occasionally at the screen.

"...As you may remember, this is the home of Willard Fisher, the Amish fanatic who killed his Amish neighbors to protect the Amish way of life. Now his son, Samuel Fisher, has been arrested for growing marijuana on this very land."

The well-groomed blonde newscaster angled her body and held out her hand to gesture to the land behind her.

"The whole situation is ironic, Jim, considering his

father killed *to preserve the Amish ways, yet his own son has turned to what the Amish would call worldly ways."*

Jake plowed his hand through his hair and sagged against the half wall that separated the TV area from the rest of the cafeteria.

"Who alerted the news?" Jake muttered to himself.

A well-coiffed man with shiny black hair filled the screen, a serious look on his face. *"Have you been able to get a comment from his stepmother, Rebecca Fisher?"*

The screen split in two and the reporter appeared again, her fingers pressed to her earpiece. *"No, Jim. Not yet. No one is home at the residence. We hope to catch Mrs. Fisher when she returns."* She smiled brightly and Jake's stomach dropped at the ghoulishness of their voyeurism.

"Excuse me," an annoyed voice came from behind Jake.

Jake glanced over his shoulder at a young woman craning her head to see around him. "Oh, sorry."

Jake checked his watch. It was getting late, but if he hurried, he could catch Rebecca at the diner before she went home for the night. He didn't want her to get a camera in her face in her front yard.

But more important, he wanted to be there for Rebecca. She might not want to admit it, but she was the closest thing to family that he had.

Tommy was behind the drugs!

Rebecca's pulse thrummed in her ears as she scrambled to find an escape. *"Please*, don't hurt me. I have two young daughters. Without me, they'll be orphans."

Rebecca clamped her jaw, trying to tamp down her rioting emotions. Willard's constant criticism and yelling had taught her to hide her feelings behind a mask of calm. She had been successful *most* of the time. She had learned to be a good Amish wife to keep peace in the home. But she had failed her children miserably.

"Go into the kitchen," Tommy said, grabbing her arm.

Using the backrest of the nearest stool to anchor herself, she shook her head. She wasn't going into the kitchen where no one could see her from the street. "No."

Tommy pulled her arm and she held tightly onto the stool with the other. Craning her neck, Rebecca glanced toward the street and her panic spiked when she realized no one was out there. No one to save her. Her fingers felt numb. She'd have to figure a way out. On her own.

For her daughters' sakes. For Samuel's. If she died, what would happen to them?

A sense of calm and determination settled over her.

"I'm not going anywhere with you."

Tommy grunted and peered around; the dark look in his eyes chipped away at her resolve.

"Tell me why you're doing this."

Tommy narrowed his gaze. "I wouldn't expect an uneducated Amish woman to understand, especially one who was stupid enough to marry the biggest loser in Apple Creek."

Rebecca sucked in a gasp. Even though she had constantly said worse in her own mind, hearing someone say it out loud was like a punch to the gut.

She hiked her chin, trying to muster a confidence she didn't feel. "Willard made his own bad decisions. I had nothing to do with it."

Tommy leaned in closer. The stale smell of coffee on his breath assaulted her nose. "He lived with you, slept in your bed and *you* didn't know what was going on?" He raised an eyebrow, a mocking glint lit his eyes.

"I didn't know what he was up to. I trusted him. Much like Professor Burke trusted you."

"Don't try to manipulate me."

The walls swayed and Rebecca sent up a silent prayer. "You'll go to jail for the rest of your life. You don't want that."

Tommy lifted an eyebrow. "Your murder will be blamed on Samuel. Poor Samuel, the son of the evil Willard Fisher. Then maybe I can put some distance between me and this mess while I figure things out."

"Samuel will tell the police you were involved with the drugs. You won't get away with it."

"*Ha.* Samuel doesn't know I'm behind it. He only knows about the Yoder brothers. And I don't suspect they'll get involved. You know how the Amish feel about law enforcement, right? And they'd have to admit their guilt. Don't see that happening. Besides, Samuel already confessed." He laughed again.

"Samuel's not even in Apple Creek. No one will blame him for this."

"I'll figure something out. I always do."

"No…" Rebecca's vision tunneled and her knees grew weak. Tommy had obviously lost his mind.

Dear Lord, help me. Give me wisdom. Let me get home to my family.

Breathe. In. Out. In. Out.

She closed her eyes briefly and Tommy came into focus. Obviously Tommy needed to be heard, otherwise he would have already hurt her. She had seen the same behavior in her husband. He liked to rant and rave and pace, forcing her to listen to his half-cocked theories. It was when she accidentally looked at him the wrong way or didn't make dinner on time that he'd lash out. He'd belittle her. Point out all her shortcomings, real or imagined.

She clung to the back of the stool tighter. "You've done

well for yourself. Why did you get involved with drugs?" She had to keep him talking.

Tommy angled his head, an unreadable expression on his face. A surge of adrenaline coursed through her. Had he sensed she was patronizing him?

"I *was* making something of myself." For a fleeting moment, he seemed smug, then his gaze snapped into focus and landed with an unnerving intensity on her. "And *you* had to ruin that." He reared back and spit in her face.

Wincing, she lifted her shoulder and wiped the spittle from her cheek.

She struggled to swallow around a parched throat. "Did you break into my house, too?"

"I was looking for a dry place for the marijuana plants. Like your basement. But you just kept interfering."

"You were in *my* home," she bit out the words. "I've never done anything to you. I don't understand."

"You wouldn't. You're satisfied with your *small* life here in Apple Creek. Working at this boring diner. You haven't been able to survive doing what your ancestors have done for years. Farm." His lips grew pinched.

"I have a family. I have young daughters. *Please.* Leave me be." She let go of the stool and ran toward the wall where Tommy had thrown the keys.

The sound of footsteps behind her made her pulse spike. *Please, God, let me escape.*

Tommy slammed her against a nearby booth, pinning her body against the cool vinyl. He squeezed her cheeks with his rough hand. She struggled to draw in a breath, yet she bit back the sting of tears. She would *not* let him see her cry.

"You *shouldn't* have done that, crazy woman."

The memory of Willard's harsh rebukes scraped across

her brain tangling with Tommy's gruff voice. His rough touch.

"You're *not* going home." Tommy lifted his hand, ready to strike her. "I'll kill you right here." She closed her eyes against the rage playing out across his features. "Your daughters will be better off without you."

The adrenaline spike made her feel both anxious and strong at the same time.

Do something! Save yourself!

Rebecca raised her arm suddenly, pushing his hand away from her face. She hip checked him and he fell on his backside, cursing her in surprise.

Rebecca bolted toward the kitchen. Her only hope now was to get to the phone on the wall next to the swinging door. She just had to dial three numbers: 9-1-1.

Icy fear pumped through her veins. Her sole focus was on the white receiver. She reached out and grabbed it.

"You ain't going anywhere." Tommy flung the phone out of her hand and it dangled by the curly cord. The distant dial tone mocked her.

Rebecca spun around and glared at him. He stopped short of slamming into her. His eyes drew into angry slits. "Because of you, I can't afford tuition. I won't be able to continue my studies. No degree means I'm going to be no better off as an outsider than I was as a Plain person." His face crumbled in rage. He grabbed her arms and squeezed. "Do you understand?"

"I understand that you've been terrorizing me to keep me quiet. To get me to stop asking questions." She thought of all the incidents of late. Her campus scare. Getting run off the road. Getting attacked not once, but twice on the farm. "You have to realize I'd do anything to protect my family. To protect Samuel. Now, *get out!*"

"If Samuel hadn't started acting all weird, you wouldn't

have started asking questions." Tommy gripped her tighter and pain shot up her arms. "I want to ruin Samuel's life like he's ruined mine."

Keep me calm, Lord. Help me. When Tommy didn't budge, she blinked back her fear and met his harsh gaze. "Take your hands off me *now.*"

Surprisingly, Tommy dropped his hands. He muttered something under his breath she didn't understand. He paced, his movements short and jerky. She eyed the keys on the floor by the wall.

"You destroyed the marijuana crops. *You* destroyed the last bit of hope I had of making money. You ruined everything that I had carefully planned. Do you know how hard it was to find a farm I could do this on? To find Uri and Jonas, who were willing to help me?"

"There have to be other ways to pay for college." Rebecca realized she was trying to reason with a young man who was past the point of reasoning.

"You would know this how?"

Rebecca took a step backward closer to the front door. "You can't do this. You can't hurt me. You'll end up in jail for life."

Tommy let out an obnoxious laugh. "Yeah, right. I'm not going to jail. And if Samuel could have played it cool after he realized the Yoder brothers had planted the marijuana, no one would have been the wiser.

"Uri and Jonas tried to bribe Samuel. Keep him quiet, but—" Tommy snorted "—I think it made him feel worse. He wasn't supposed to have worldly things. They warned him to keep his mouth shut or bad things could happen. He went over the edge after Elmer died. Stupid kid. Then you started in with the questions."

"Tommy, it's over now." Rebecca kept her tone calm. "You must take responsibility."

"No." Rage vibrated off him. "I refuse to be a nobody. Without an education, without a good job, I will be as invisible as all the Plain people in this community."

"You are not invisible," Rebecca pleaded.

Tommy glanced down, then reached for something under the counter. The silverware bin.

Rebecca grew lightheaded.

Tommy reached into the gray container, grabbed a steak knife and held it out to her in a menacing gesture. "Move into the kitchen. *Now.*"

Rebecca slowly shook her head. "Please, I have children. Katie. Grace. You've met them. I'm all they have."

Tommy's face scrunched up and he shook his head quickly, as if he were trying to dismiss a bad taste. His features smoothed over and he held the knife low near her side. "You will *not* use Amish guilt on me. I am not Amish."

A knocking startled her. Tommy snapped his gaze toward the door and fear flashed in his eyes.

"It's Jake," she breathed, relief and fear tangling in her stomach.

Tommy let out a mirthless laugh. "Jake, huh? Figures."

"He's not going away."

Tommy lowered the knife to hide it below the counter. There was a chance Jake hadn't seen Tommy or if he had seen him, he wouldn't realize what was going on.

Jake knocked again, this time more urgently.

"Let me answer it," Rebecca whispered. "It's time we ended this."

Tommy looked discreetly down at the sharp knife pointed at her delicate midsection. "Wave him off. Tell him to go home."

Rebecca did as she was told, waving to Jake to go on home. *I have to finish up here*, she mouthed.

Every movement, every word, every motion shifted into slow motion. Rebecca felt as if she was having an out-of-body experience.

The door rattled as Jake tried to get in. "He's suspicious." Her mind raced. "Let me get the door, please. I'll get rid of him." She decided to change tactics.

"I'm not stupid. You have no reason to get rid of him."

"I love Jake. I don't want him to get hurt."

Tommy's eyes flashed dark and he tilted his chin toward the door. "Answer it. Tell him I'm here interviewing you for a research paper."

Rebecca opened her eyes wide, a spark of hope igniting in her chest. "Okay, I will. But...what if he wants to talk to you?"

Tommy has nothing to lose.

"If you tell him what's going on, I'll kill him, then track down your daughters at your brother's house and kill them, too."

All the blood rushed to her head and heat swept over her. Each tic of the clock was amplified in her ears. "How do you know where my daughters are?"

He lifted a knowing eyebrow. He must have heard her talking to Flo.

"I'll get rid of him." Tears bit at the back of her eyes, but she refused to cry. She cautiously walked over to the floor where her keys had been thrown. She picked them up and moved toward the door. She startled when Tommy came up behind her.

"I'll be right by your side." He put the hand with the knife on her back and they moved as a unit toward the door.

The pressure of the knife at her back made her dizzy with fear. Staring at the lock and not meeting Jake's curious gaze through the glass door, she inserted the key, turned the lock and opened the door a fraction.

When Jake reached the diner, the door was locked but he saw Rebecca and Tommy in what looked like a heated discussion behind the counter. His brow furrowed with curiosity.

What's Tommy doing here?

Something felt…off.

Jake knocked on the glass door and both Tommy and Rebecca jumped. Something was definitely off.

When they continued to talk without coming to the door, he pounded on it. This time harder. He didn't know what was going on, but he knew he had to get in there.

Rebecca waved at him to dismiss him and if he was being honest with himself, it hurt. She wasn't even going to talk to him?

"I need to talk to you." Jake shook the handle of the door. "Please open up."

Rebecca glanced over her shoulder. If Jake hadn't been watching her closely, he might have missed the worry in her brown eyes.

Adrenaline surged through his veins. "Unlock the door, Rebecca!"

Rebecca picked something up off the floor, then walked toward the door with Tommy right behind her. Jake tried to get her attention, but all her focus was on the door lock.

Tommy gave him a half smile, but something in Tommy's eyes made Jake pause.

Rebecca pulled open the door a fraction, but she didn't invite him in.

"Hi, Jake. Did you need something?" The stiff set of her shoulders confirmed his suspicions.

"I'll drive you home." He decided he could tell her about

the news crews in front of her home once they got into the car.

"I'll drive her home," Tommy said casually. "Mrs. Fisher is answering some questions for my research paper."

Jake's gaze moved from Tommy to Rebecca and back. "Is everything okay?"

"*Yah*. Tommy promised me it wouldn't take long." Jake thought he detected a shudder in her breath.

"Not long at all. Then I'll make sure she gets home," Tommy said.

"Are you sure?" Jake put his palm on the door.

"*Yah*, it's fine. Please go."

Jake leaned in close. "Are you okay? You look pale." He reached out to touch her arm and she blinked slowly, not answering him.

Jake pushed the door open and Tommy stepped back, a knife in his hand. The knot in Jake's stomach twisted. He reached out to grab Rebecca, to pull her out of the way, but Tommy was faster. He grabbed Rebecca around her neck and held the knife against her cheek.

Jake lifted his hands in a surrender gesture. "Don't hurt her. Whatever's going on, I can help you."

Beads of sweat glistened on Tommy's forehead as he gritted his teeth. "If the two of you hadn't stuck your noses where they didn't belong... I needed to sell the drugs to pay tuition. Who was I hurting?"

Tommy yanked Rebecca's head back and she gasped. Her brown eyes widened with fear. A single tear rolled down her cheek.

Tommy was not going to let her go.

"Hurting Rebecca won't solve your problems." Jake slowly took a step forward while Tommy walked backward.

"Killing Rebecca would have been justice. Justice for everything she took away from me."

Rebecca groaned as Tommy tightened his hold.

"Let her go. It's no longer about Rebecca. I'm here, too. You'll have to kill us both."

Tommy smirked, as if he had already figured that out.

Anger bubbled in Jake's gut. Someone had really messed Tommy up.

"I'm not going to be easy to take down." All of Jake's senses went on high alert.

"I'll take my chances." Tommy continued his backward motion toward the door leading into the kitchen. He gave a quick glance over his shoulder and adjusted his direction. "I'm not going to live as a jobless nobody… And I'm not going to prison."

Jake tried reasoning again. "We could have found ways to pay your college tuition without resorting to drugs. We *can* still find a way."

Tommy's laugh grated across Jake's brain. "Yeah, right. I'm sure the financial aid office—which is already useless—will give *me* a scholarship. Perhaps from the pool of scholarships for convicted felons."

Jake fisted his hands. "You haven't done anything too serious yet. Hurt Rebecca and all bets are off."

"There's no going back." Tommy's voice shook with fury. He pulled Rebecca back with him and she flinched. He reached the swinging door and tripped backward over the lip on the floor.

Rebecca reached out and Jake grabbed her arm, pulling her away from Tommy, who had fallen onto his backside. Jake pushed Rebecca out of the way and swung into action. His army training all coming back to him.

Jake kicked the knife out of Tommy's hand. It spun across the linoleum floor and disappeared under the stove. The young man scrambled to his feet and Jake slammed him into the wall.

"It's over," Jake said. "It's over." He met Rebecca's gaze as she collapsed onto a nearby counter stool and bowed her head.

SIXTEEN

Jake held Tommy's arms firmly behind his back while Rebecca called the sheriff. She stood by the doorway to the kitchen, as if she were ready to take flight if Tommy escaped his grasp.

That wasn't going to happen.

"How could you do this?" Jake asked Tommy. "I trusted you. The young Amish men who talked to us trusted you."

"An opportunity to make some easy cash. I couldn't refuse. Tuition is expensive," Tommy said, his tone flat and distant, as if he were replaying the choices he had made over the past year.

"The cash didn't come easily, did it?"

When Tommy didn't answer, Jake pushed Tommy's cheek into the wallpaper that had probably been there since the 1950s. Tommy groaned. Straining his neck to glare at Jake over his shoulder, Tommy said, "What does it matter now? My future's ruined."

"Don't be too rough." At some point Rebecca had moved next to them.

"Yeah, listen to the lady," Tommy said, full of snark and authority.

Rebecca's gaze drifted to the door. "Here's the sheriff."

Sheriff Maxwell strode into the room, curiosity in his

gaze. Jake and Rebecca explained what had happened and the sheriff took Tommy away in handcuffs.

Rebecca collapsed onto the stool and put her hand on her forehead.

Jake walked over to her side and grabbed the back of the stool, even though he really wanted to pull her into an embrace. Thank God he'd arrived when he had. He glanced around at the people milling about outside and he knew a hug wouldn't be appropriate.

"Are you okay?" he asked, squeezing the back of the chair. He wanted to push a loose strand of hair behind her ear.

When it came to Rebecca, he was definitely in trouble.

"I am now." She swallowed hard. "What brought you to the diner tonight? If you hadn't come by…" She shivered and wrapped her arms around her middle.

Jake ran a hand across the back of his neck. He hated to bring Rebecca any more bad news.

She must have read it in his eyes. "Tell me. It can't be worse than this."

"The TV was on in the student union on campus. There's a news crew in front of your house. I wanted to make sure you didn't have to face them alone."

Rebecca's forehead furrowed. "News crew? From the television. Why?"

"Someone must have alerted them about Samuel's arrest, so they set up on the road in front of your farm."

"How did they find out?"

"They have ways. They might have seen his name on a police report and wondered if he was related to Willard."

"Fisher is a common Amish name," she said. "It would have been a leap to make the connection."

"Maybe it was Tommy," Jake suggested.

"Yes, it had to have been. He told me he was going to

make it look like Samuel had killed me." Rebecca covered her mouth, bowed her head and whispered, "I could have been killed tonight…and my daughters wouldn't have had a *mem*."

"I'll never let anything happen to you." The words came out of his mouth before he had a chance to think how they would affect Rebecca.

She looked up at him with watery eyes. She covered his hand with hers, then quickly pulled it away and placed it in her lap.

"I didn't mean to add to your stress tonight." Jake smiled. "We can discuss our relationship at another time."

Rebecca blinked slowly. "Tommy told me Samuel was innocent. He wanted to rub it in my face that I'd never be able to tell anyone."

Tommy had been willing to kill her.

"Do you think Tommy's confession will be enough to bring Samuel home? To untangle this mess?"

"We can talk to the sheriff. It'll definitely be a good start."

Jake slipped his arm around her back and helped her stand. "I'm going to take you home."

Rebecca looked up at him. "Thank you. I can't thank you enough."

Jake brushed his thumb across her cheek. "Thank God I was here."

Rebecca touched his arm. "Can we pick up Katie and Grace before you drive me home? I need to see them."

"Of course." With a hand to the small of her back, he escorted her to his vehicle parked along the curb out front.

Jake parked his truck sideways in front of her house, blocking the view of the front door from the news truck. Rebecca ran ahead with the girls and unlocked the door while Jake walked down to the street and asked the crew to leave.

Rebecca closed the door behind her and drew in a deep breath. The scent of an old fire in the stove and a hint of peppers from breakfast reached her nose. *Home.* She had never been more grateful to be home than she was tonight.

She bent and drew her daughters into a hug. The Amish weren't big on physical displays of affection, but tonight Rebecca would make an exception. She might have never seen her daughters again if Tommy had had his way.

"Are you girls hungry?" Rebecca asked.

"*Neh*," Katie answered.

Grace shook her head. "Maybe Katie can read me more of *Little House on the Prairie*."

"*Yah*," Katie said without hesitation. "I want to know what happens next."

Rebecca placed her hands on their heads. "Well, okay. But instead of going up to your room, stay down here." Rebecca wanted the company of her daughters after everything she had been through.

Katie ran upstairs for the book and then the two girls settled in the rockers in the sitting room. Rebecca went into the kitchen to put on some water for tea as she listened to Katie read to her little sister. Her heart was full.

A moment later, Jake slipped into the kitchen. "The news crew is packing up. I called the sheriff. He promised them a statement if they came down to the station. He also promised them a photo op with Tommy if they hurried."

"A photo op?" Rebecca repeated, confused.

"Bottom line, they're gone. I also told the sheriff about Tommy's statement that Samuel was innocent. They'll work on Tommy. See if they can get an official statement."

Rebecca closed her eyes and felt the weight lifting from her chest. "Thank you again."

In the privacy of the kitchen, Jake took her two hands in his. "I'm glad I was there for you. We are both truly blessed."

Rebecca felt her cheeks heat and she turned her face away. She could still hear Katie's soft voice reading to her sister. "After everything that happened with Willard, and then Samuel, I had often felt uncomfortable in my own home. But tonight, when I realized I might never get to return, I realized that a house doesn't make a home. It's the people." She lifted her eyes to meet his. "Oh, listen to me ramble on." She shook her head and smiled up at him. "I'm happy to be home with my daughters."

She met his gaze and with a burst of courage she didn't know she had, she said, "I'm glad you're here, too."

He pressed a kiss to her forehead and her heart expanded.

Then with even more courage she said, "I'm never leaving the Amish. If you want to become Amish, you need to do it because it's best for you. I don't want you to resent the decision."

Jake dragged the tie of her bonnet through his fingers. "You talked about home. I've never felt more at home than when I'm with you."

Her pulse beat steadily in her ears. The voice of her daughter faded off into the distance.

"My parents left the Amish in search of something else," Jake said. "I've been searching all my life for someplace to belong. The army. College. Through my research. But I always felt at a distance." He pointed to his chest. "I know my place is with you." He grazed her cheek with the back of his hand. "I need to be baptized to court you."

All the world disappeared and the only thing she could see was his handsome face. She wanted to tell him once again that if he joined the Amish it had to be for his own reasons. Not for her. But she couldn't get the words out.

Knowing this warm, compassionate man had tender feelings toward her made her heart soar. He brushed a soft kiss across her lips and whispered, "Wait for me."

EPILOGUE

Sixteen months later...

"Why didn't *Mem* go ice-skating with us?" Katie asked as she held out her arms and did a shaky twirl.

Jake skated over to her, ready to catch her if she hit a rough patch on the frozen pond. "I suppose she had other things to do."

Grace skated toward them with short choppy steps. Jake had been working with the girls for an hour each day, ever since the pond had safely frozen over two weeks ago.

"Maybe *Mem*'ll have hot chocolate waiting for us," Grace said, her words came out on an icy puff of air. She clapped her blue mittens and said, "I'm cold."

"How about you, Katie? Ready to go in?" Jake squinted against the flurries. The sun low in the sky reflected off an ominous, gunmetal cloud in the distance. "Looks like more snow is on the way."

"No school!" Katie said as she glided to the edge of the pond.

Jake smiled. Some things were universal.

It took a few minutes for the three of them to change from their skates into their boots. Jake had set up a little wooden bench by the edge of the water for just this purpose. He had grown to love the simplicity of life since quitting his job at the university and becoming Amish. He worked the land and built things, and he finally had time to work on a book about the Amish he had long been planning. He wasn't sure how the church elders would feel about that, but he figured he'd present it to them before he published it.

He vowed to show the Amish in the best possible light while also sharing some of their struggles. Struggles that were real. The Yoder brothers were currently both in prison for their involvement in aiding Tommy in his drug venture. Tommy was in prison, too, but his sentence was much longer. Maybe there would be a role for someone like Jake to work with young Amish men who wrestled with the decisions facing them as they moved into adulthood, bridging the gap between the Amish world and the one outside.

"Last one to the house is a rotten egg," Grace hollered as soon as she had slipped on her second boot. She was off like a shot over the fields to the tiny dot that was his home now.

Katie rolled her eyes as she tied the laces of her skates together and hiked them up on her shoulder. "Let her run ahead. I don't really care if I'm a rotten egg." She smiled, and it reminded him of his Rebecca.

The two walked across the field, their boots crunching the snow underneath. "We might have to put snowshoes on next time we come out here. It's really starting to snow."

When they reached the steps, Katie slowed down and looked up at him. She had yet to hit her teenage years, but every so often, in her mannerisms, he detected a hint of the woman she was becoming.

"*Denki* for being nice to me and my little sister."

Jake's chest tightened. "Of course." How could he be anything but to these two precious girls?

"My *dat* was very strict and made my sister and me afraid. It's just…" She seemed to be struggling with the words. "It's nice to have peace in the home."

"Yes, it is." He held out his hand, encouraging her to go ahead of him, but she paused.

"Is it okay if Grace and I call you *Dat*?" Katie glanced down and drew circles in the freshly fallen snow with her boot. "Grace and I have talked about it, but we wanted to ask first. You and *Mem are* married and everything."

A knot formed in Jake's throat. "Of course, I'd like that."

"Okay, then." Katie slipped the ties of her skates off her shoulder and hustled inside.

Jake turned and canvased the land. God's land. He was truly home.

The door swung open and Grace ran in, leaving a trail of wet puddles from the snow in her wake.

"Slow down there," Rebecca admonished.

Grace stopped and smiled, panting. "Katie's a rotten egg."

"Oh, stop that. No one's a rotten egg." Rebecca couldn't help but smile. This past year had brought much happiness to her little family. Jake had followed through and had been baptized this past summer. They were married in October, as soon as the harvest season was over. Now a few months later they had settled into a nice routine.

The only time Rebecca went to the diner now was to meet her friend Hannah for lunch. It was also nice to catch up with Flo. Jake had saved up some money, allowing Rebecca to stay home with the girls on the farm, and allowing them to plan for the future. Meanwhile, Jake had thrown himself into working the farm the summer before their marriage and truly seemed satisfied with it. Now in the dead of winter, he spent his time with the family and his writing.

Rebecca had feared he'd regret becoming Amish, but he truly seemed at peace.

The door opened again and Katie stepped in, followed by Jake. He smiled at her and her heart fluttered, a reaction only his smile inspired. They all took off their winter gear and settled around the heating stove.

"*Mem*, you should come skating with us tomorrow. I want to show you how I can skate," Grace said, rubbing her hands together near the stove. "Can you come with us?"

Rebecca looked up, meeting Jake's eyes. "I don't know if that's such a good idea." She placed her hand on her belly. She had felt sick this past week, but after a quick visit to the doctor today, she knew for certain.

Over the heads of their two daughters, Jake raised his eyebrows. *Really?* he mouthed.

Love expanding in her chest, Rebecca nodded. Jake closed the distance between them and pulled her into a tight embrace.

She closed her eyes and breathed in his scent, the fresh smell of soap mixed with the great outdoors. When she opened her eyes, Katie and Grace were staring up at them with curiosity.

With his arm still wrapped around his wife, Jake placed his other hand on her belly, an intimate gesture reserved for husband and wife. He met her gaze, getting her unspoken approval.

"Katie, Grace," he said, "how would you like to have a baby brother or sister?"

They both scrambled to their feet and came to their mother's side. "Is it true?" Katie asked, always the more conservative of the two.

Rebecca reached out and cupped her eldest daughter's cheek. "Yes, honey. Are you happy?"

Katie nodded, but her lower lip quivered.

"What's wrong?" Rebecca whispered.

Jake put a hand on Katie's shoulder.

"I'm happy."

"Then why are you crying?" Grace asked in the way only little sisters can.

Rebecca brushed away the tears with her thumb. "Those are happy tears."

Katie nodded. "I can't wait to tell Samuel. When will we see him? He gets to be a big brother again."

"He and Marian are coming for a visit next week if the weather's good."

After all the drug charges had been dropped, Samuel had remained near Rochester in an Amish district in communion with Apple Creek. He'd been baptized around the same time as Jake and had married a pleasant Amish girl from a big family there.

"I hope the weather's good," Grace said.

Rebecca gently tapped her daughters' bonnets. "You girls warm up and I'll make you hot chocolate."

Katie and Grace held up their palms to the heating stove.

Jake wrapped his arms around Rebecca and whispered into her neck. "You make me the happiest man alive." A warm tingle ran down her spine.

Her face flushed. She'd never get used to Jake's warm affection. Some of his outsider ways were welcomed. She held her hand to his chest. "I need to make hot chocolate."

Slowly he shook his head. "*Neh*, sit." His hand brushed her stomach. "I'll make some for everyone."

Reluctantly, Rebecca relaxed and picked up her knitting.

She watched as Jake walked into the kitchen. He glanced over his shoulder and smiled at her.

A warm feeling swirled around her heart. Love. Happiness. Contentment.

And peace.

Most definitely peace.

* * * * *

Dear Reader,

Welcome back to Apple Creek, New York. I hope you enjoyed Rebecca's story. If you read my previous Harlequin Love Inspired Suspense, *Plain Peril*, you'll recognize Rebecca. She played a secondary role and when she first walked onto the page, I never anticipated making her the heroine of her own story. When it came time to plot a new Amish story, Rebecca wouldn't leave me alone. I guess she decided she needed her own happily-ever-after. I hope you agree. (Rest assured, you can read and enjoy *Plain Threats* without having read *Plain Peril*, but if you want to know more about Rebecca's backstory, check out *Plain Peril*.)

When I started writing, I never envisioned I'd produce so many Amish stories. However, I've grown to love my Amish friends in Apple Creek. Crafting an inspirational romantic suspense has a set of expectations and constraints. Tossing Amish into the mix creates even more challenges. Fun challenges. These challenges generate inherent conflict. Conflict is key to a good story. I hope you've enjoyed *Plain Threats*. If you want to read more about Apple Creek, please consider checking out *Plain Pursuit* and *Plain Peril*.

As a reader, what draws you to Amish fiction? I'd love to hear from you via email at Alison@AlisonStone.com or you can write to me at Alison Stone, P.O. Box 333, Buffalo, NY 14051.

Live, Love, Laugh,

Alison Stone

REQUEST YOUR FREE BOOKS!

2 FREE RIVETING INSPIRATIONAL NOVELS
PLUS 2 FREE MYSTERY GIFTS

Love Inspired®

SUSPENSE
RIVETING INSPIRATIONAL ROMANCE

YES! Please send me 2 FREE Love Inspired® Suspense novels and my 2 FREE mystery gifts (gifts are worth about $10). After receiving them, if I don't wish to receive any more books, I can return the shipping statement marked "cancel." If I don't cancel, I will receive 4 brand-new novels every month and be billed just $4.99 per book in the U.S. or $5.49 per book in Canada. That's a savings of at least 17% off the cover price. It's quite a bargain! Shipping and handling is just 50¢ per book in the U.S. and 75¢ per book in Canada.* I understand that accepting the 2 free books and gifts places me under no obligation to buy anything. I can always return a shipment and cancel at any time. Even if I never buy another book, the two free books and gifts are mine to keep forever.

123/323 IDN GH5Z

Name	(PLEASE PRINT)

Address	Apt. #

City	State/Prov.	Zip/Postal Code

Signature (if under 18, a parent or guardian must sign)

Mail to the **Reader Service:**
IN U.S.A.: P.O. Box 1867, Buffalo, NY 14240-1867
IN CANADA: P.O. Box 609, Fort Erie, Ontario L2A 5X3

**Are you a current subscriber to Love Inspired® Suspense books
and want to receive the larger-print edition?
Call 1-800-873-8635 or visit www.ReaderService.com.**

* Terms and prices subject to change without notice. Prices do not include applicable taxes. Sales tax applicable in N.Y. Canadian residents will be charged applicable taxes. Offer not valid in Quebec. This offer is limited to one order per household. Not valid for current subscribers to Love Inspired Suspense books. All orders subject to credit approval. Credit or debit balances in a customer's account(s) may be offset by any other outstanding balance owed by or to the customer. Please allow 4 to 6 weeks for delivery. Offer available while quantities last.

Your Privacy—The Reader Service is committed to protecting your privacy. Our Privacy Policy is available online at www.ReaderService.com or upon request from the Reader Service.
We make a portion of our mailing list available to reputable third parties that offer products we believe may interest you. If you prefer that we not exchange your name with third parties, or if you wish to clarify or modify your communication preferences, please visit us at www.ReaderService.com/consumerschoice or write to us at Reader Service Preference Service, P.O. Box 9062, Buffalo, NY 14240-9062. Include your complete name and address.

LIS15

SPECIAL EXCERPT FROM

Love Inspired®

Will a young Amish widow's life change when her brother-in-law arrives unexpectedly at her farm?

Read on for a sneak preview of
THE AMISH MOTHER
The second book in the brand-new trilogy
LANCASTER COURTSHIPS

"You're living here with the children," Zack said. *"Alone?"*

"This is our home." Lizzie faced him, a petite woman whose auburn hair suddenly appeared as if streaked with various shades of reds under the autumn sun. Her vivid green eyes and young, innocent face made her seem vulnerable, but she must be a strong woman if she could manage all seven of his nieces and nephews—and stand defiantly before him as she was now without backing down. He felt a glimmer of admiration for her.

"*Koom.* We're about to have our midday meal. Join us. You must have come a long way." She bit her lip as she briefly met his gaze.

Zack still couldn't believe that Abraham was dead. His older brother had been only thirty-five years old. "What happened to my *brooder*?"

Lizzie went pale. "He fell," she said in a choked voice, "from the barn loft." He saw her hands clutch at the hem of her apron. "He broke his neck and died instantly."

Zack felt shaken by the mental image. "I'm sorry. I know it's hard." He, too, felt the loss. It hurt to realize that he'd never see Abraham again.

LIEXP0915R

"He was a *goot* man." She didn't look at him when she bent to pick up her basket, then straightened. "Are you coming in?" she asked as she finally met his gaze.

He nodded and then followed her as she started toward the house. He was surprised to see her uneven gait as she walked ahead of him, as if she'd injured her leg and limped because of the pain. "Lizzie, are *ya* hurt?" he asked compassionately.

She halted, then faced him with her chin tilted high, her eyes less than warm. "I'm not hurt," she said crisply. "I'm a cripple." And with that, she turned away and continued toward the house, leaving him to follow her.

Zack studied her back with mixed feelings. Concern. Worry. Uneasiness. He frowned as he watched her struggle to open the door. He stopped himself from helping, sensing that she wouldn't be pleased. Could a crippled, young nineteen-year-old woman raise a passel of *kinner* alone?

Don't miss
THE AMISH MOTHER *by Rebecca Kertz,*
available October 2015 wherever
Love Inspired® books and ebooks are sold.

Turn your love of reading into rewards you'll love with

Harlequin My Rewards

**Join for FREE today at
www.HarlequinMyRewards.com**

Earn **FREE BOOKS** of your choice.

Experience **EXCLUSIVE OFFERS** and contests.

Enjoy **BOOK RECOMMENDATIONS**
selected just for you.

PLUS! Sign up now
and get **500** points
right away!

Earn
**FREE
REWARDS**
Join
Today!
HarlequinMyRewards.com

MYR16R